MW00387476

MAKING HAY

PAMELA MORSI

CHAPTER 1

"Then it's settled. You two will marry as soon as the hay is in." Widow Nora Green smiled across the table at the serious faces of her daughter, Lessy, and her soon to be son-in-law, Vassar Muldrow. "I'm just so tickled I could purely swoon," she added. "And I know, Vass, that your mother and daddy will be just as delighted."

The big, blond young man gave a slight nod of agreement and stole a careful, respectful glance toward his future bride. "They couldn't be more delighted than me, ma'am."

Four years earlier, when Nora's husband, Tom, had died, Vassar Muldrow, the youngest son of a distant cousin from Arkadelphia, had come to help out on the Green farm. It had been a good thing for all concerned, and from the first day the widow had held secret hopes of a match. Hopes that had now materialized.

"You can't be calling me ma'am anymore." Nora Green was beaming. "It just ain't family sounding. You just call me Mammy, like Lessy does." She nodded firmly. "You call me Mammy Green."

Vassar's smile was broad and friendly. He was a quiet and serious young man; the widow saw his smiles rarely, but considered them worth the wait. The wide slant of his mouth and the seemingly small brilliant white teeth made his rather plain farmboy face glow with good looks. "I'd be honored, Mammy Green."

"What kind of wedding are you wanting?" She looked fondly at her only child.

Her daughter, just turned twenty, sat demurely across the table from Vassar. Her pale brow hair was parted very straight down the middle, each side tightly braided and rolled into two carefully secured swirls at the back of each ear. Excitement glittered in her eyes, but she held tightly on the reins of her enthusiasm.

"I don't think we need a big to-do," she told her mother quietly. "I think if we just get the preacher to marry us on the church steps after service, then we could come back here for the wedding supper."

Nora Green frowned slightly. "That ain't much

of a wedding, honey. You sure you don't want something fancy and grand? I've got a little money saved up, and a girl only gets married oncet."

Lessy cast a glance at Vass that seemed almost hopeful. His look was open and unassuming, but she shook her head. "There's no need to pull a fuss," she said with a lightness that didn't fool her mother for one minute. "You save your money, Mammy, for something important. We'll be just as married without some showy shindig. Vass and I are quiet people."

If the widow's murmur of assent didn't quite ring true, it was clear that Vassar's nod of approval was all that Lessy noticed.

"I just want you to be happy," her mother said.

Both young people turned to look at her curiously, as if it had never occurred to them that they wouldn't.

"Do you want more pie or coffee?" Lessy asked her young man.

Vass shook his head and patted his belly with contentment. "I couldn't eat another bite."

Lessy rose to help with the dishes, but her mother waved her away. "I'll wash up these things. You two are officially engaged." She smiled warmly at Vass. "I think that means you can go walking out with my daughter alone now."

Vassar's cheeks reddened, and he appeared

more ill at ease about the prospect than delighted. "Do you want to walk out with me?" he asked Lessy.

She blushed also as she nodded her agreement. With roses in her cheeks and sparkles in her eyes, her rather ordinary appearance blossomed to genuine comeliness. Vass looked away.

Helping her out of her chair, he offered his arm like a swain at a dance. Lessy took it, her expression blissful. As the widow watched them step out onto the front porch, she shook her head.

There was something about this engagement that wasn't exactly right.

A HALF MOON WAS RISING IN THE EASTERN SKY and turning the hot summer evening silver gray in its light. The young couple strolled casually from the front porch of the farmhouse down the path that led past the corncrib, into the peach orchard, and toward the pond.

"It's a pretty night." Lessy took a deep breath. The warm summer scent of ripening fields and maturing fruit always pleased her, but tonight it could have been pouring rain, and she would have been happy. Her spirit soared within her.

Vass nodded as he surveyed the fleeting light critically. "The weather's been just about perfect this year. Com and oats were good, the stock is near fat enough for market, and your peach trees are still producing when they were nearly to breaking limbs with fruit a full month ago."

Smiling, Lessy agreed. "It's been a very good year." She gave him a shy glance. "I just hope that's a good omen for a wedding."

Vassar kept the serious gaze of his pale blue eyes straight ahead. "We don't need any omens, Lessy. We've had four years of getting to know each other. This is not some dizzy craziness that will pass with the first rough row to hoe. There aren't many couples who are as sure of wanting a marriage as we are."

"Of course, you're right." Looking up at him, Lessy's heart was in her eyes.

She felt as dizzy and crazy as the first day they'd met. Vass was big and blond and tanned ruddy from working in the Arkansas sunshine day after day. And his long, thickly muscled arm so close to her own was strong and warm, even through the thin covering of his near-threadbare cotton shirt.

Vass glanced down at her and gave her a small smile of encouragement before he looked away, assessing the grove around him and the fields farther on.

'The hay is about ready," he said. "I wrung out a

handful today, and it broke near as clean as celery. I suspect to get the haying crew up here any day now."

"That soon?" Lessy asked.

Vass nodded. "If the weather holds, we'll have it all in the barn in three weeks' time."

"So I guess we should plan on the wedding about the end of the month."

It was a statement, but she looked up at Vassar as if it were a question.

"Sounds fine," he answered. "I'm glad we're just having a quick marry-up."

Lessy cleared her throat and nodded determinedly. "A big wedding does seem like a waste of money."

"More than that. It's sure a kind of foolishness for a couple such as us. It isn't like marriage is going to be a big change in our lives."

Lessy raised her eyes in surprise.

"I mean, of course it's a change," Vass hastily corrected himself. "But it's ... well... you're not leaving home, and I'll not be working a new farm. Our lives will be pretty much what they've been for the last four years." Lessy made no reply, but Vass noticed her biting her lip nervously and tried again to explain. "You'll go on doing what you do every day," he said. "And I'll go on doing what I do. Things will be just the same. Except, of course, that we'll be a ... a . . . sharing a room." Vass rubbed his palms nervously against his trouser legs.

Her face flushing bright crimson, Lessy could only nod in reply. Vass took her speechlessness as concern.

"Now, please don't start to worry about that, Lessy," he said. "I promise it won't be as bad as you're thinking." She looked up curiously, but when she met his eyes, she dropped her gaze again in embarrassment. Vassar gently patted her hand.

"I want children as much as any other man," he told her quietly. He swallowed and looked away from the woman beside him. Once again he felt a twinge of regret. She was sweet and innocent and deserved a better man than he. "I'll try not to bother you excessively."

"I know you won't," Lessy whispered, her face flaming with humiliation.

They hurried on, as if moving out of the fragrant peach orchard would move their thoughts into new directions as well. When they reached the edge of the pond, they could go no farther. Both of them stared out over the water, wistfully, as if wishing for the courage to look at each other.

Lessy's grandfather had dammed up a small creek when he'd first arrived in this part of Arkansas. The pond was so well established now, only those who knew it was man-made could distinguish it from a natural water hole.

A spindly willow tree grew on the bank, and the couple stopped beneath it. Vassar leaned against the tree trunk as Lessy gazed out over the water listening to the croak of the frogs and the rattle of crickets. He no longer held her arm.

"Have you thought what you want to do with your peach money this year?"

She smiled, grateful that he'd introduced a safe subject for discussion. The peach orchard had been Grandma Green's pride and joy, and she'd willed it separately to Lessy. Since she was a little girl, every year that the peaches made money, Lessy spent it on whatever she pleased.

"Mammy and I thought we could send for some dress silk from the catalog. Mammy says a woman needs something new to get married in." In her mind she could picture herself in a beautiful gown, Vass standing beside her... perhaps looking at her proudly ...

When he made no further comment, Lessy finally asked, "What do you think I should do?"

He shrugged. "I was thinking we might could raise some birds on this pond. A few ducks and geese wouldn't be much of a worry. And there ain't nothing like a big old fat goose in the roasting pan."

A vision of her dreamed-of silk gown fluttered into oblivion. “Then waterfowl it is. Mammy and I can make over one of the dresses that I already have.”

“You really don’t even need nothing new since you’re marrying me,” he said. “I think you look mighty pretty in your regular Sunday-go-to-meeting.”

Her regret over the loss of a wedding dress was soothed by the compliment. Vass made so few. Lessy was pleased as she glanced over at Vassar. He was grinning and pulled himself to his feet. Moving to stand in front of her, he took her hands in his own.

It got very quiet between them as they both stared at their clasped hands. Vassar looked away and took a deep breath before turning back to her.

“With us betrothed now,” he said, “I guess a kiss would be in order.”

Lessy smoothed a wispy lock of hair that had escaped the tightly twisted braids and raised her chin bravely. “Yes, I suppose that would be all right.”

With only a slight hesitance Vassar leaned closer. Gently, oh, so gently, he pressed his mouth against the soft, rosy cushion of her lips. Lessy inhaled the raw, sweet scent of him and felt the heat of his nearness. The soft touch of his lips was so brief, barely lingering, over almost as soon as it began.

Vassar stepped back, ran a nervous hand through his hair, and cleared his throat. "We'd best get back to the house. Your Mammy will be worried."

THE WIDOW GREEN DID NOT APPEAR TO BE THE least bit worried when Lessy returned home. Her mother was sorting through the wardrobe in their bedroom and humming pleasantly to herself.

"Mammy? What are you up to?"

With a gesture toward the sorted clothes strewn across the bed, she answered, "I just thought I'd get some of this packing done before the haying crew arrives and we get so busy."

"Packing?" Lessy plopped on the side of the bed, her expression puzzled. "Are you going somewhere?"

Nora Green looked up and shook her head, chuckling. "Did you think I'd expect you to move into the little room with Vass?"

Lessy hadn't thought about it at all.

"Of course you two should have the front bedroom," she said. "It was meant for a married couple."

Lessy glanced around uneasily at the room she

had shared with her mother for the last four years. It suddenly seemed a strange and alien place. When she'd imagined sharing a room with Vassar, she'd always seen herself crossing the threshold of the little one added onto the back of the house where she'd spent her childhood. It had been Vassar's room since the day he had come to live with them. It was almost as if she couldn't remember a time when he hadn't been there.

"We wouldn't want to run you out of this room," she protested. "This is the room you shared with Daddy." Widow Green reached out for her daughter's hand. "It was, indeed, the room I shared with my husband, and it will be the room you share with yours."

A mixture of delight and anxiety skittered inside Lessy, and she averted her eyes.

She had wanted to marry Vassar Muldrow since the first day that she had seen him, a few weeks after her father's death. She was sad and scared and confused. Although she had always been close with her mother, Daddy was so very special. He'd called her Gopher-Girl for her love of gardening, tree planting, and any other dirt-digging activities. And he'd given her confidence in herself.

"You can be anything you want to be, Gopher-Girl. Your life is like a batch of your mama's bread dough. You can shape it into a standard loaf, twist it into curlicues, or you can tie it into sailor knots. It's all up to you."

Lessy had smiled at him skeptically. "I suppose I can make my hair blond and my eyes blue and turn into Sugie Jo Mouwers if I want."

Her father had raised his eyebrows in surprise at the mention of the exuberant young daughter of one of the neighboring farmers. "I don't doubt that you could if you put your mind to it," he'd said. "But I hate to see you aiming so low."

"Aiming so low?"

Tom Green nodded thoughtfully. "Poor Sugie Jo is a ray of sunshine in a very dark, brooding family. That's a burden that merely being *pretty* ain't going to overcome. You, Gopher-Girl, should be thinking about your own life. You have the chance to be whatever your heart desires. You've just got to figure out what you want in this world."

And she had. She wanted Vassar Muldrow.

That first summer after they'd laid her beloved father in the ground, Cousin Jake and his sons had shown up to help harvest the cowpeas. She could remember, as if the image were burned into her brain, her first look at Vassar Muldrow. He was standing in the back of the wagon unloading their gear. His golden-blond hair seemed almost burnished in the sunlight, and his tall, broad-shouldered physique made him appear a giant of a man.

Heartsore and lonely for the man who called her Gopher-Girl, Lessy needed the strength she'd seen in those young shoulders and was drawn to the pain in those murky green eyes that seemed to mirror her own.

"Nora, this is my youngest boy," Jake had said to her mother as he gestured to Vass. "He's the one I wrote you about. He ain't much one for talking, but he's a good hand and a hard worker."

Vass had glanced in their direction and given them an excessively polite nod of acknowledgment.

Lessy had felt a catch in her throat and a jolt in her heart. He doesn't *have* to talk, Lessy thought to herself. I'll be happy to do his talking for him.

Her sigh of sweet remembrance caught her mother's attention.

"Lessy-mine, you're not worried about sharing a bed with this man, are you?"

Her cheeks pinking only slightly, Lessy shook her head.

"No, Mammy," she said. "I've been around the farm long enough to know pretty much what happens. And Vass says it won't be as bad as I think."

Her mother's mouth dropped open in surprise before she threw her head back and laughed. "Lord-a-mighty, you and Vass are the strangest pair of cooing doves I ever laid eyes on. Not as bad as you think?" The Widow Green shook her head in disbelief.

"Is it that funny?" Lessy asked, unable to keep the hint of pique out of her voice.

Nora reached over and patted her hand affectionately. "No, honey, you know I wouldn't make fun of you or Vass. You are both the dearest to me on this earth. But I swear you two have the oddest ideas of courting that I've ever come across in all my born days."

Lessy raised her chin, still slightly defensive. Their courting had been unique. In fact, it had been like no courting at all. Vass never wooed her or sent her flowers or carried her to a barn dance or church supper. He was a shy man and didn't like social occasions. Although Lessy had once reveled in carefree fun and meeting with friends, she now only wanted to do what Vassar wanted to do. And what Vassar wanted to do was farm.

"It's normal for you to be a little scared of your marriage bed," Lessy's mother was telling her. "And it's right for Vass to try to reassure you. But, I'll swanny, he has a strange way of going about it."

Lessy didn't want to talk about Vass. "Did Daddy have to reassure you?"

Nora Green nodded. "He surely did. I was three years younger than you are and had been so sheltered I thought the difference in men and women was the clothes that they wore."

Lessy laughed and shook her head, refusing to believe her mother's claim.

"I was scared near to death," her mother told her. "But when your daddy realized why, he snuck me down behind that big old barn at Granny's place and kissed me till I was breathless. I was so het up, I told him I didn't want to wait even one more day. It was only your daddy's good sense that kept us from making our marriage bed in that damp grass."

"Oh, Mammy!" Lessy giggled. "I can't imagine you and Daddy sparking behind the barn."

"Well, it's the truth." Her eyes were soft with the memory. "But if you tell it at church, I'll deny every word." Nora Green pointed her finger at her daughter threateningly, and both dissolved in laughter. "If my memory serves me right," her mother continued when they'd regained composure, "these warm summer days can fire up a young man's blood and a young woman's, too. Many a young couple have met the preacher *coming back* from the well. More than one have lived to regret it. I never heard tell of a pair that were sorry they'd waited till the wedding day."

Lessy leaned forward and hugged her mother

tightly. "Don't worry, Mammy," she said. "There is not even a question. Vass and I are going to wait."

Nora looked at her daughter for a long moment and then nodded in agreement. "I guess I should know that. Vassar is a mother's dream. He's polite, respectful, honorable, and upright. But when a man's in love, it'd be hard to fault him for stealing a kiss or two."

Lessy's smile held, but the pleasure behind it faded, and she lowered her eyes to the cotton petticoat that she held in her hands.

CHAPTER 2

The singing woke him. Every morning, as regularly as the sunrise or the cock's crow, Lessy Green sang as she stoked the fire in the stove and set coffee to boil. Today it was a cheery but subdued "On the Banks of the Ohio." Vassar was just grateful it wasn't 'Ta-Ra-Ra- Boom-De-Ay"!

Without opening his eyes, he sluggishly rolled to a sitting position on the side of the bed. His feet touched the cold boards on the floor.

I am awake, he told himself.

He allowed his left eye to open to a squint. With a moan he closed it again, and only pure strength of will kept him from falling backward onto the bed.

Vassar hated mornings.

"It's the devil's own laziness in that boy!" one of his aunts had told his mother. "Never heard of a farmer who didn't love the first light of day."

Vass didn't know if he loved it. He tried very hard not to see it.

The gentle tapping on the door diverted his attention from his own weariness, and he blindly rose to his feet and felt his way across the room.

He pulled open the door wide enough only to reveal his face.

"Good morning, Vassar. It's a beautiful day outside. Breakfast should be ready in about twenty minutes."

The sweet shy voice held a revitalizing power, and Vassar obligingly opened his eyes fully for the first time. Lessy stood, fresh-scrubbed and pink, in his doorway. The neat braids on either side of her head were precise and perfect.

THE PLAIN CALICO WORK DRESS SHE WORE HAD been carefully pressed to best advantage, and the sun-bleached apron tied around her waist was as clean and neat as lye soap and a washboard could make it.

"Morning." His voice was deep and gravelly.

Vassar took the pitcher of warm water she offered, and with a nod that he hoped conveyed his thanks, he shut the door. Then he staggered to the washstand. He poured the water into the basin and set the pitcher aside before bracing himself with both hands and leaning toward the spotted shaving mirror. He grimaced at the wavy reflection he saw there. Farming would be a better line of work if it didn't start quite so early in the morning.

He closed his eyes once more and almost managed to fall asleep again standing up. His own swaying motion startled him awake, and he looked at his reflection in the mirror with distaste. "Lazy slugabed!" he accused. His tone held real anger and self-disgust. Like most men, Vass had weaknesses. But unlike most, Vass knew that his own failings, his own flaws, had and could cause infinite pain and unending regrets. His own weakness had ruined lives, innocent lives and guilty ones, also. Since coming to the Greens', he'd determined never to let his weakness show again. So, leaning forward, he scooped a double handful of the warm water and splashed it on his face. Like it or not, the days started early in Arkansas.

By the time he made it to the kitchen, at least he'd begun to look more like a hardworking farmer than a rounder after a wild Saturday night.

Lessy was alone, still sweetly singing. Without a word to her, Vassar reached for the pristine bucket that hung by the chum. Lessy glanced over at him, a warmth of pride lighting her face.

"Oh, I've already done the milking."

Vassar gave a grunt of acknowledgment before he hung the bucket back on its nail. He looked on top of the cupboard to see the elm splint gathering basket was missing.

"Eggs?" he asked.

"Mammy's gathering them now," Lessy answered.

He nodded with gratitude and regret. He was late again. What must Lessy think of the man she'd agreed to marry? Milking was surely his task. And although many women gathered their eggs, his father had always both milked and gathered while Mama cooked breakfast.

With a mild feeling of failure Vass seated himself at the table, his pride in shambles. Lessy was perfect. A perfect woman destined to be a perfect farm wife. He eyed her as she bustled about. Cheerful and steady, Lessy's hardworking life and happy disposition shamed him. Leaning his elbows on the table's edge, he put his head in his hands. He rubbed his eyes to try to dispel the lassitude that still lingered there, but he could easily have drifted off again had Lessy not set a mug of steaming hot coffee in front of him.

"Thanks," he muttered.

He took a sip as Lessy moved to put the biscuits beside him, singing again.

She had a pretty voice, and Vass was grateful for it. But how could anyone be so dang cheerful at daybreak! The screen door slammed as Nora Green returned.

"Best get that breakfast on the table, Lessy," she said before turning her attention to Vass. "I saw a dustcloud out to the west—bet it's the haying crew coming down the road."

Vass made to rise, but the widow stayed him. "You can't be putting in a day's work on an empty stomach."

Agreeably Vassar accepted the plate of bacon, biscuits, and grits Lessy set before him. "How many eggs do you want?" she asked.

"Give him a half dozen," Nora answered for him. 'That's a big man you've got to fill up, Lessy, and a long day ahead of him."

Vass was wide awake when the haying crew led by Roscoe Doobervale pulled up into the yard. Roscoe had been doing business at the Greens' farm since before Lessy was born. He was a fellow of about Mammy Green's age and sported a bushy gray mustache that seemed constantly in need of trimming.

"Blessed day to you, Vassar," was the older man's greeting.

"Looks like a blessed day for hay cutting, if you're ready."

Roscoe nodded and gestured toward the men who were just beginning to jump down from the back of the hay wagon where their gear was stowed. Trailing behind the wagon, like stray dogs following a sausage truck, were the machines that made modem haying a quick and reasonable task for a half dozen men. Vass immediately found his steps leading him to the shiny mechanical wonders. Almost with reverence he gently caressed the cold, brightly painted metal of the rake bars.

"You know most of these boys," Roscoe said, interrupting Vass's communion with the farm implements.

Looking up hastily, dismayed at his own bad manners, Vass acknowledged the men in the crew who were familiar to him. "John, Angus, Claidon."

Handshakes were exchanged.

"That boy is Angus's," Roscoe said, pointing at a ruddy- complexioned young man in his teens. "His name's Tommy. And this here is Ripley. He's quite a hand with the machinery. He's got that newfangled haykicker of mine slipping through the fields like a knife through butter."

A man in his mid-twenties jumped from the back of the wagon. There was a sauntering laziness to his walk, but no shortage of implied power in his thick muscular arms and thighs. His coal-black hair hung in loose curls around his head, and bright blue eyes gazed out of a strong, handsome face. He gave a friendly nod to Vass, his smile was broad and his teeth straight and white, and one long, deep dimple curved down his left cheek. The new man was only a few inches shorter than Vassar and had to look up only slightly to meet his gaze. After wiping his hand casually on his trousers, he accepted the offered handshake. Vassar's huge bearlike paw was much bigger than Ripley's own, but his grip was of a man to his equal.

"Pleasure to meet you, Mr. Green. You got some fine good fields a-growing here."

"The name's Muldrow, Vassar Muldrow." He glanced around with pride. "I grew the fields, but they aren't mine. The Widow Green owns this place."

Ripley nodded with polite apology at his mistake and then raised a teasing eyebrow as he glanced around at the other men. "Widow, huh? I'm right partial to widows." His words brought a guffaw of laughter from the rest of the crew. Vass felt vaguely unsettled.

"That Ripley's got him a gal on every farm we've been through this year," John Crenshaw explained. "I suspect half the gals in Arkansas are expecting him to come back at the end of the season and put a ring on their finger."

Those words brought a spurt of laughter from the crew.

Vassar grinned companionably with the rest.

Old Roscoe shook his head with disapproval. "There's more truth to that than I want to think about."

"I swear I don't know how he does it," John said. "He just smiles that pretty smile and talks some pretty talk, and them gals are clinging to him like ivy on bramble vines."

Ripley shrugged with feigned innocence and chuckled good-naturedly.

Vass was grinning more easily now. "I hope you don't set your sights on Widow Green. She ain't much of a woman for foolishness. My daddy sent me here for her to straighten out my ways. You start talking pretty to her, and she's liable to wash your mouth out with soap."

Ripley nodded, his words open and friendly. "Thank you, Muldrow. I consider myself warned. And call me Rip—everybody does."

Vass slapped Rip on the back.

It took the better part of the morning to unload all the equipment. The crew would be camping out near the hay barn, where they could shelter in case of inclement weather.

Vass began hitching up the teams to the equipment and found Ripley at his side. He'd already noticed the man had a good mind for tools and implements as well as a quick wit. Rip had kept up a steady stream of conversation, which more than once brought a blush to Vass's cheek and a grin to his lips.

" ... and so the Quaker stood back a moment and recovered himself, and then he reached over and patted that mean old milk cow on the flank and said, 'Nay, Bossy, I shall not strike thee. But on the morrow I'll sell thee to a Baptist, and he'll beat the hell out of thee!' "

Vass chuckled at the image and shook his head. But as he reached over to take the tie from Ripley, he saw the young man's gaze was looking past him.

"Well, well," the handsome young man drawled with a grin. "The widow might not be quite my style, but that one with her would be *worth* getting a mouth washing for."

Curiously Vass turned to see Mammy Green and Lessy setting up the dinner table in the yard beside the house.

"That young one will do me just fine," Rip was saying. "I ain't close enough to see if she's pretty, but she's got a handsome way about her. See how she moves. It's like her feet don't touch the ground at all."

Following Ripley's gaze, Vassar watched Lessy walking around the table. It *was* kind of an interesting walk. He'd never noticed it before.

'That's Lessy. Widow Green's daughter."

Rip's grin widened. "Her daughter? You've been holding out on me, Muldrow. Dirty Devils awaiting, I'll be slicking my hair back when I go a-sparking her."

Words sticking strangely in his throat, Vass finally managed to cough out a curt reply. "Miss Green is my intended."

Ripley turned his attention back to Vass. His eyebrows were raised in surprise before he grinned wryly and with a feigned look of disgust folded his arms belligerently across his chest. "Well, if that ain't a jackass pa-toot! Why didn't you say so in the first place? You let me get my hopes all up and then tell me the gal is claimed. You warning me off?"

Vassar scoffed and shook his head as he hooked the traces to the crupper. "There's no need for 'warning you off,' Ripley. Lessy is a quiet, hard-working woman without a thought in her head for flirting or vanity."

Rip raised a speculative eyebrow. 'Two peas in a pod, hey?"

Vass shrugged. "More like two sheaves of grain," he said. "We've grown up together these last four years and have common goals for ourselves and the farm. We have a shared past and have expectation for a shared fate."

"A shared fate?" Ripley whistled with admiration. "Now, I've told a gal or two that we were *destiny,* but I sure never made it sound as doggone boring as you do."

Vass felt stung. "Maybe my Lessy *likes* boring."

Ripley shook his head. "The gal may like *you,* but they ain't *no* gals that like boring."

THE PLATTER OF FRIED CHICKEN WAS SO HEAVY IT took both Lessy and her mother to carry it. Feeding seven working men was a chore, and the two had started cooking the midday meal as soon as Vass had left from breakfast.

"Is that everything?" Lessy asked, surveying the heavily laden table.

"Good graces, I've forgot the bread!" Widow Green exclaimed. "Go call the hands to dinner and bring those loaves on your way back."

Lessy hurried to the back porch and clanged the triangle loudly with the wand that hung from it by a string. With only a hasty glance toward the men near the bam, she stepped into the kitchen to get the bread. Six perfectly brown crusty loaves, still warm from the oven, were already piled in a wicker basket. She grabbed it up, but before hurrying out, she hastily checked her reflection in the small looking glass imbedded into the inlay of her mother's china cabinet. Her hair was still in place, but she smoothed it nonetheless. Her brown eyes were big, too big she thought, and too close together to be truly attractive, but she didn't really mind. Her nose, however, was thin and straight and sharp. Without thinking, she tapped the end of it with her index finger, a habit she'd formed years ago when Sugie Joe had told her that it came to a point like a butcher knife.

Reassured, Lessy let her fingers drift to the underside of her lower left jaw. A bout with smallpox as a youngster had left three small craters there that never shrank even after being massaged with cream treatments or browned with sun. Vassar was too kind to have ever mentioned the marks.

With a determined huff, she fought back the wave of self-pity that had churned up inside her. In fact, Vass really never commented on her appearance. Vass was not a man to be lured with a pretty face or charmed by vain foolishness, she mused. There was no flour on her nose or grease splatters on the bib front of her apron. She was clean and neat. That was all a good woman was expected to be. Raising her chin with determined pride, she headed out to the table spread under the maple tree.

Vass had already seated himself at the head of the table when Lessy set the basket of bread in front of him. He looked up and smiled. Her heart lifted with the flash of his white teeth, and shyly she returned his grin with one of her own.

Clearing his throat, he placed his elbows on either side of his plate and clasped his hands together before laying his forehead against the knuckles. "God, our blessed Father," he began.

Lessy squeezed her eyes together tightly and sent up the silent prayer that she offered so frequently these days. *Thank you for sending me Vass. Help me to be the wife that he needs.*

When Vassar offered a deep baritone amen, Roscoe seconded it loudly, and the table of men eagerly reached for the bowls of food within their grasp.

Scrutinizing the contents of the table once more, Lessy nodded reassuringly to her mother seated at the end of the table before picking up a pitcher of ice water to fill the goblets on the table.

"Lessy, you remember Roscoe," her mother said, gesturing to the older man on Vassar's right. Lessy gave him a welcoming nod. "It's good to see you, Mr. Doobervale."

Widow Green introduced the rest of the crew

to her daughter as Lessy filled their glasses and politely repeated their names. When Lessy made her way around the table to the young man at her left, he turned to her and offered his hand.

"Ripley, ma'am," he said. His eyes were bright blue and warm with laughter as he looked at her.

Rather awkwardly Lessy transferred the pitcher from her right to her left hand before offering hers. Glancing down, she saw her palm was damp from the coolness of the water she carried. Self-consciously she pulled it back and wiped it on her apron, then flustered with embarrassment, she offered her hand once more. The young man did not, as she expected, give her a hearty handshake, but merely grasped her long slim fingers in his own and gave them a most delicate squeeze.

"What a delight to meet you, Miss Green," he said, his eyes twinkling as they looked straight into hers.

"Nice to meet you, too, Mr. Ripley," Lessy replied. She was slightly taken aback by the warmth of his greeting and a little concerned that he still held her hand.

"Please, call me Rip," he said, dropping his voice ever so slightly. "You are Miss Lessy, I believe. May I be permitted to address you by your given name?"

His formal question seemed so out of character

with his flirtatious tone that Lessy almost giggled. "That would be fine."

"Lessy." He repeated the name slowly, thoughtfully, rolling the s's off his tongue in a caressing way. "It is a diminutive of Celesta, I presume."

"Why, yes."

Ripley cocked his head slightly to one side and let his eyes explore her head and shoulders. "Celesta. It means heavenly, you know."

She nodded slightly.

His tone softened with warmth. "And the name does suit you ... Lessy."

A strange something skittered across her stomach at the unexpected compliment. She felt immediately ill at ease and fought the desire to drop the water pitcher at his feet and hide her unheavenly face from his gaze. Purposefully collecting herself, she leaned forward slightly to pour water into Ripley's goblet. She felt somehow safer with her hands at work until she cast a glance at the handsome young man only to catch him eyeing her bosom. With a nervous start she jerked back from the table, managing to spill a very cold dollop of water on Rip's trousers.

"Oh, I'm sorry!"

Ripley wiped at the water on his thigh and gave her a careless gesture of unconcern. "I suspect I needed a little cooling off."

His remark brought a snorty chuckle from the youngster across the table from him.

Lessy's eyes were immediately drawn to Vass. He sat silently at the head of the table watching the byplay, his green eyes looking at her in a way she found strange and unfamiliar. She felt suddenly as embarrassed and exposed as if wind had thrown her skirts over her head and her best drawers had been in the wash. Their eyes caught, and she blushed and looked away.

Glancing down at the man beside her, Rip's bright smile was open and friendly. The stranger seemed to offer a safe haven from new feelings that were distinctly uncomfortable.

As if in apology for some slight he'd caused, Ripley turned his attention to his plate, and Lessy moved on down the table to fill the glasses of John Crenshaw and Claidon Biggs, before taking her place to the left of Vassar.

"Muldrow tells me you are about to become his bride," Ripley said.

Blushing, she spared a hasty glance toward Vass. "Yes." Her voice was a shy whisper. "As soon as the hay is in."

Rip's smile broadened into a grin as he looked around the table. 'Then I pity this crew," he said. "With a lovely bride like Miss Lessy awaiting, Muldrow will drive us like Missouri mules!"

The men around the table chuckled. Rip gave Vass a challenging grin. Staring back at him silently, Vass continued to chew his food.

"What about you, Mr. Ripley?" Lessy asked. "Have you got a wife or a sweetheart waiting for the end of the season?"

Tommy McFadden laughed loudly this time with the less than delicate enthusiasm of youth. "Rip's too smart to fall into some gal's trap!"

Lessy raised her eyebrows in surprise at the words; Ripley just gave a shrug.

"I just haven't found that right woman, Miss Lessy," he said. His smile widened and his expression softened. "Seems every time I meet a girl I could think about marrying"—he turned to glance down the table meaningfully at Vassar—"some other fellow's already claimed her." Lessy's cheeks sparkled with bright warm color at his implied compliment. What a rogue he was! And what a gentleman. She smiled with shy pleasure at Ripley for a timid moment before grabbing up the basket before her and offering it across the table. "You didn't get any bread, Mr. Ripley. I baked this myself, and some say I've quite a knack for it."

CHAPTER 3

The sky was still an inky blue as Lessy made her way out to the barn to milk. Vass had said he would tend to the cow this morning, but she hated to wake him. And with seven men to feed in addition to her regular chores, she wanted to get an early start on the day. Mammy was helping, of course. But she was letting Lessy lead, giving her a chance to prove what a good farm wife she could be. Lessy welcomed the chance. She wanted Vass to be proud of her.

She let herself into the door of the barn, and the sweet, warm smells of clover and alfalfa assailed her. Like everything else on the farm, the barn was nearly as clean as a church. Vassar believed that cleanliness being next to Godliness meant animals and farm buildings as well as personal hygiene.

"Morning, Sissy," she said to the big buff-colored Guernsey that stood in the first stall. Lessy quickly gathered up some feed for the cow, and stepping past her in the stall, scattered it evenly in the trough. Sissy wasn't willing to wait as Lessy neatly spread her morning meal. She pushed her big, anxious head up under Lessy's arm, trying to push her out of the way.

"For shame, Sissy!" Lessy scolded her as she patted the cow sternly on the cheek. "A lady has got to learn some patience at the breakfast table."

Sissy's reply was a loud unconvinced moo.

"You going to sing with me this morning?" Lessy gave the cow one loving caress on the flank before she left her to her eating and gathered up her stool and pail. She hummed a tune that was playing in her head, though she didn't know the words. It was a sweet, light tune, cheery and fresh, a tune Vass often hummed. She thought of it as Vassar's song. It made her feel close to him to hear the sweet sounds coming from her own lips.

Lessy heard the crackle of hay underfoot only a moment before a fine tenor voice joined in her song.

"Millie's brother's gunning for me,
And the fault is mine, they say.

She lost her drawers at the Sunday School picnic.

And I'll ne'er regret that day."

"What are you singing!" Lessy's eyes were wide with shock as she stared at Ripley leaning indolently against the stall post.

Rip's grin was wide, his eyes were bright, and his stance was teasing, hands in his pockets, arms folded across his chest. "You were the one humming the tune," he said. "I just joined in with the chorus."

"But those words, I—" Lessy sputtered, her face flaming with embarrassment.

"At least I only sang the chorus," he said. "Why, the verses of that naughty ditty would put kinks in your hair faster than a curling iron!"

Lessy's face was fiery red. "I didn't know the words," she protested.

Rip folded his hands in front of him and surveyed the blushing young woman before him. His lips twitched and his eyes danced, but his tone was gentle. "It's a drinking song, Miss Lessy. You hear it bellowed by a hoard of galoots at the top of their lungs when they're out on a round. It's called 'Plowing Millie.' "

It seemed impossible that Lessy's eyes could get any bigger, but they did. She nearly choked on her own words. “Oh, dear,” she began. “Mr. Ripley, I never—well, I really didn’t... I—”

Rip held up a hand to silence her. “I’m sorry I embarrassed you, Miss Lessy. I heard your sweet voice humming that wicked little tune, and I just had to join in. I shouldn’t have let you know the words.”

“Oh, no,” Lessy assured him. “I am very grateful that you did. I hum that tune quite often, and I certainly ... well, I wouldn’t want anyone to ... to, well... to get the wrong idea.”

Rip hunkered down in the stall next to her and smiled with genuine admiration. “Miss Lessy, nobody would get the wrong idea about a woman like you,” he said. “You are sweet and warm, and when you give your heart to a man, he’d never have cause to doubt.”

Lessy smiled, her face flushed with pleasure. “Well, Mr. Ripley, that is certainly a glowing endorsement.”

“Every word of it is true.”

“You don’t even know me.”

“I know enough.” His voice was a low gruff whisper. ‘Things about you just shine on through. I know that you are strictly the marrying kind.”

Lessy turned her attention back to the cow. “Well, aren’t most women?” she said. “And I am to be married shortly.”

"Yes, that's what I hear. And I certainly envy Muldrow his good fortune."

Lessy turned to look at him. Surprised and puzzled at his words, she was not sure if they were not just flattery.

Before she could make a determination, Rip's fingers reached out to lightly trace the curve of her jaw and tenderly caressed the tiny white circles he found there.

"I know what these are," he said.

Lessy pushed his fingers away. "They're pockmarks."

"Pockmarks!" Rip sounded horrified. "No, ma'am," he said firmly. "I'm absolutely sure this is where the fairies kiss you in the dead of night."

She giggled. "No fairies are kissing me in the dead of night."

"No? Maybe it's Muldrow." He hesitated a moment and touched the tiny scars again before his voice dropped to a husky whisper. "Lucky Muldrow."

A tiny whimper of surprise and shock escaped Lessy's lips as a strange tingly feeling emanated from his hands to her flesh and throughout her body. Her pulse jumped and a covey of butterflies took flight in her stomach. Her hands stilled at their work. She did not so much as blink, feeling frozen in place.

Her eyes wide, Lessy stared at the handsome man beside her who was looking at her in a way no one had before. She could feel the depths of heat in his eyes, and ripples of anxious excitement quaked through her body.

Vassar! Her mind whispered his name as a plea. The trembling inside her made her think only of Vassar.

The heavy humid silence between them held for one full minute.

Sissy made a noisy complaint and stamped her hind foot threateningly. Lessy jumped slightly, startled. The cow's interruption broke the spell, and she jerked away from the warm male hand that caressed her.

"Mr. Ripley, please."

He immediately withdrew and made apology. "Forgive me, Miss Lessy," he said. "Morning and mockingbirds always get the best of me. They get the best of any man, I suspect."

Lessy wondered.

His words were made with such a boyish sincerity and an impish grin that her discomfiture ceased immediately, and she found herself smiling and shaking her head at him. He was flirting with her. The idea of a handsome young man making pretty talk to a plain farm woman that was practically married filled her with delight.

"I've got no time for foolishness this morning," she said. "I've got a big breakfast to get on the table and a whole day's chores to do."

His grin widened. "Don't let me stop you, Miss Lessy. It's my ambition to one day marry myself a right-living farm gal and watch her a-working all day long."

Lessy threw him a look of mock exasperation as he chuckled and leaned indolently against the stall. Contentedly she continued her milking with his eyes upon her.

"So do you flirt with all the women you meet?" she asked him.

Clutching his hand to his chest dramatically, he assured her that it was not so. "Not all the women, certainly," he said. "Just most of them."

In response Lessy turned the teat she held in her hand in his direction and squirted the toe of his workboot with warm milk.

Rip raised his hand like a captured criminal. "Don't shoot, ma'am. I'm unarmed."

When the milk was just foaming along the top of the pail, Lessy pulled it out of Sissy's way and handed it to Rip.

"Don't spill it," she admonished him as if he were a youngster.

"I'll do my best, Miss Lessy," he assured her.

She hung the three-legged milking stool on the

side of the stall before leading Sissy out the back of the bam. Lessy removed her halter and gave the milk cow a grateful slap on the rump.

"See you at sundown, Sissy."

With lazy grace Sissy leisurely strolled away from the barn without so much as a backward glance and began her morning inspection of the pasture.

Lessy watched her for a minute before turning back to Rip, who stood in the doorway, milk pail in hand.

"I can take that now," she told him as she came back into the barn.

"It would be my pleasure to carry it for you, Miss Lessy," Rip answered with a flourish of his hand indicating that she should lead the way to the farmhouse.

The two were laughing together as they stepped into the back door of the farmhouse. Vass was leaning against the cupboard, coffee cup in hand, but with his eyes closed. At the sound of their entrance, he stood up straight as an arrow and stared in surprise.

"Good morning, Vass," Lessy said sweetly. "You're up early."

"Morning, Muldrow," Ripley said. "Where do you want this milk, Miss Lessy?"

Lessy turned her attention back to him. "Let

me get the cheesecloth, and you can strain it into the milk can."

VASS WATCHED THEM WORK WITH A STRANGE catch in his heart. "You're up early, Ripley," he said.

The young man smiled at him, his straight white teeth glimmering in the dim morning light of the kitchen. "I'm an early riser," he said. "I can hardly wait for the days to begin."

Vass took a large swig of coffee and winced as it burned his mouth. He had tried to be an early riser this morning. He'd forced himself out of bed at the first cock's crow. But apparently it hadn't been early enough. Ripley had already been slicked up milking and laughing with Lessy before he'd even got both eyes properly opened.

"Stop that or I'll hit you with a frying pan!" Vass heard Lessy warning. Turning toward them, he saw Rip with the last bit of milk in the pail threatening to douse Lessy.

'Turnabout is fair play," Ripley stated, his eyes bright with mischief. "You squirted milk on me—I pour it on you."

"Not if you want biscuits."

"Ah, biscuits." Rip's grin widened. "Quick bread made from your sweet hands, Miss Lessy, would taste to me like manna from heaven."

Lessy giggled with delight. Her pink cheeks and bright smile were very alluring.

Vass cleared his throat uncomfortably. A stab of hot jealousy seared his heart. She and Rip looked so happy together. Their talk was soft and flirty. Vass envied that talk.

But it could never be that way for him, he admonished himself. He respected Lessy too much. Vass would never risk the loss of control a flirtation might provoke. Other men could play with fire, but Vassar's own carnality had already burned too many.

THE MOWER CUT A WIDE SWATH TOWARD THE right of the wheels as it moved across the meadow. John Crenshaw sat high above the team, pulling a line as straight as an arrow. In front of him, Roscoe and Vass walked through the knee-high grass, searching the ground for hidden dangers to horse or cutting blade. Behind the mower Claidon Biggs, Angus McFadden, and his son stirred the worst of the cutting with rakes. The hay would have to be fluffed and separated to dry. The haykicker would do most of that, but still hand labor could spot a potential problem that might break a rake spine and set men and machinery back a day or more.

At a distance Ripley drove the haykicker. He

stood on the crossbar, reins in hand, as he guided the shiny piece of farm equipment into the cutting. The haykicker scooped the hay from the ground with spikes and tossed it into a wooden cagelike bin. The bin, connected to the wheels, tumbled the grass over and over as it moved, getting both sunlight and breeze into it. Sometimes known as a tedder, the haykicker took the place of dozens of women and children who in days long past would have been asked to follow the mower or scythe and toss and shake the cut by hand. The newfangled modern machine was able to stir the grass and then evenly spread it against the ground to dry in neat windrows. Fresh-cut hay would not be safe stored in a bam. Damp grass took to rotting and became as combustible as kerosene on a fire grate.

From the shade of the front porch Lessy watched their progress as she shucked corn. Squinting, she could almost make out Vass in the distance. His familiar straw hat hid his face from view, but the breadth of his shoulders made him easily distinguishable from the others.

Grabbing up the next ear of corn, she clasped the husk at the blackened tip of the silks and ripped it down with one swift, smooth motion. Snapping off the stem, she pulled the rest of the husk with it and began stripping down the fine silks that clung so tenaciously to the ridge rows.

She wanted Vassar Muldrow. For four years now she had wanted him more than anything in her life, and she'd gone after him with everything she had.

Within days of his arrival on the farm, Lessy had known that he was a serious-minded worker. He had no time for frolic or foolishness. It was as if he held his fears and feelings in fine leather harness with a sharp steel bit to pull up when necessary. Lessy admired his control and emulated his example. But her heart cried that there was more behind his stern facade. That the pain behind his eyes was real and raw and that surely she could soothe it.

But he would never let her close. He would never let anyone close who threatened the restraint that bound him. Lessy understood almost immediately that like catching a chicken in the henhouse, to catch Vassar Muldrow she must scratch as hard and crow as loud.

Lessy was, by nature, neither quiet nor thoughtful. She loved life in a way that she couldn't quite tamp down. A warm, open girl, she loved to laugh, to run, to sing in the sweet air of morning and the purple shadows of closing day. She had been a high-spirited child who ran wild through the meadows and climbed every tree in the orchard. But overnight she had become a quiet young lady of decorum and responsibilities. A lady that Vassar Muldrow might want to marry.

And the change had not gone unnoticed. Her mother's brow was furrowed more than once over the metamorphosis. The people at church assumed it was her father's death that "calmed young Lessy down." But she thought that her mother knew the truth. The truth that love had conquered Lessy Green.

It had been an improvement, Lessy thought to herself. It had been time for her to grow up and assume the dignity of womanhood. She would have done so, sooner or later, had Vassar not arrived. But since he had, there was no reason why she couldn't take it on in a way that was calculated to please him.

Watching young Vass, Lessy had come to know him. He *looked* at Sugie Jo Mouwers. But he was more comfortable talking to Maizie Watson, the preacher's wife. He played dominoes and chinkerchecks, but he preferred to spend his evenings reading the *Farm Bulletin.* He could sing quite fair and was light on his feet at the local dances. But he was happier walking the land and humming to himself.

Lessy watched and had learned. She was now as easy to talk to as the preacher's wife, totally content with an evening of reading, and openly stated her preference for farm activities over social outings.

In point of fact, Lessy did love the farming and had never dreamed of a different life. But though she'd become everything Vass wanted, for four long years Vass had fought the love that she offered.

Having plucked the last stringy thread of cornsilk from the roasting ear, Lessy threw it into the basin and grabbed another from the basket.

Now Lessy had won him at last. Their marriage was only weeks away. And she and Vass were now perfectly matched.

Grabbing the dark husk tips of corn, she ripped down with her usual efficiency. She gave a startled little cry and dropped the ear abruptly. A big, furry green and brown corn borer lazily crawled along an eaten-out path of kernels. She shuddered slightly before determinedly jerking up the corn and flicking the hideous worm into the pile of husks bound for the compost heap. She hated creepy, crawly things, especially corn borers. It was amazing how they could hide so completely in what appeared to be a perfectly developed ear of corn.

Lessy snapped off the wormy piece and threw it in the husk pile before she cleaned the silk out of the untouched portion and continued her work.

Again she gazed across the fields to the hay meadow. The haykicker made its noisy way behind the men and mower, and Lessy's eyes were drawn to it. Her lips widened to a smile.

That Ripley was about the best-looking fellow she'd ever seen in her life. And with his pretty face came a silver tongue. That man could talk snakes into buying shoes. Her memory strayed to the touch of his hand on her cheek. She tutted to her self and shook her head. Clearly, Mr. Ripley had a way about him that was likely fatal to the female sex.

Ripping open another ear of corn, this time more hesitantly, fearing more corn borers, she absently wished that Vass had some of those winning ways. Then she forcibly pushed the thought from her mind. If Vass was not the romantic type, then the romantic type was not what she wanted.

CHAPTER 4

It was full dark before Vass stepped in through the back door.

"You still at it?" he asked of Lessy, who was noisily puttering about the kitchen.

She shook her head and smiled at him warmly. "I'm just getting a little ahead for tomorrow. Mammy's already gone to bed, and I was really waiting up for you."

Clearing his throat uncomfortably, Vass cast a nervous glance toward the bedroom Lessy shared with her mother. Being alone with her was surely asking for trouble.

"You want to go walking out?" The question was asked almost incredulously. Everybody on the farm had been working almost nonstop since daybreak, and the whole crew was bone tired. If Vass didn't go to sleep now, he wouldn't be able to rise until noon tomorrow.

"Oh no," Lessy assured him quickly. "I know you're tired, and... well, the barnyard and the orchard don't seem quite our own with the hay crew staying there."

Vass nodded in agreement.

"I'd just like to sit in the parlor a few minutes if you'd like to," Lessy said. "Perhaps we could just visit a little, tell each other about our day."

Tiredness aside, an unchaperoned evening in the parlor was something that Vass knew he should discourage. Still, they were betrothed, and a few moments of his time during a busy working day seemed such a simple request.

Vassar nodded. Lessy was more precious to him than anything he'd ever worked for in his life. She deserved heaven on earth, he was sure of that. Unfortunately, he had a lot less to offer. If she wanted a bit of companionship, it was certainly his duty as well as his pleasure to provide it.

Stimulating conversation, however, was not one of Vassar's strong points, and as the two settled themselves on opposite ends of Mammy Green's brocatele divan, he began his usual turn of phrase.

"Did you see that new haykicker out there? Is that some kind of machine or what? I'd be sitting pretty with a piece like that hitched behind my team."

"It's a very fancy machine," Lessy agreed.

"We got a lot done today."

"Oh?"

"Yep. If it keeps up this way, we may be done by the end of the week."

'That's wonderful."

As the subject concluded, a long pause ensued.

"How are the hens laying?" he asked finally.

"Only nine this morning," she answered. "But you know how much they hate this heat."

"Hmmph," Vass agreed. "What about Sissy—she don't look to go dry?"

Lessy shook her head. "Sissy's just fine. She seems to be in the prime of health. I think she spends the hot afternoons sitting down in that shady spot in the little creek."

"Umph," he agreed. "I saw the garden as I came in. It looks plenty big still. You've got enough tomatoes out there to feed the Arkansas Guard."

Lessy smiled warmly and tilted her head to give him a welcoming look. "I know how much you love tomatoes."

Vass smiled back, his face flushed with pleasure, and cleared his throat absently.

'The peach orchard looks—"

"Vass." Lessy interrupted him gently. In her

mind's eye she saw the corn borer inside what looked to be a perfect roasting ear. "Let's talk about something else."

"Something else?"

"Something else besides the farm. That's all we ever talk about, it seems. We just talk about the farm. Why don't we talk about something else tonight."

"Well, sure, Lessy," he agreed. "We can talk about whatever you want."

The two sat smiling silently together for a long moment. "Sure hope this weather holds," Vassar blurted out finally.

Lessy nodded. Silence.

"There's talk at church about a harvest revival," she said.

Vass nodded. Silence.

"I see your mother is fixing to switch rooms with me." Silence. Lessy blushed furiously, and Vassar coughed, mentally kicking himself in the head.

The room became quiet once more. Vass scanned the ceiling boards as if topics for conversation might be written upon them.

"Roscoe told me that he and his wife took the train to Kansas City last year," he said finally.

"Oh, really?"

"Um-hum. He said they just drove the buggy up

to DeQueen to catch the train, then sat back and watched two states go by from their window."

Lessy sighed. "That sounds wonderful."

"You like traveling?"

She giggled. "I wouldn't know," she told him. "I've never been anywhere."

Vass smiled. "Well, I don't care for it much. It's a lot of heat and bother, and I like sleeping in my own bed. But maybe we could go up to a stock show or something sometime. Just so you could say you've been somewhere."

"Oh, no, please," Lessy said. "I wouldn't want to go just for me. If you don't like traveling, then we'll just stay here."

His expression softening, Vass reached over to take her hand and squeezed it gently. "Sweet Lessy, I believe you are a sainted angel that God sent to me.".

He ascribed the vivid blush that swept her cheeks to modesty. Lessy seemed disconcerted, giving him quick encouraging little smiles and then dropping her gaze to her hands.

Vass searched his brain for lighter topics. Perhaps they could discuss last Sunday's sermon. Unfortunately, he didn't remember a word of it. He grabbed upon and then discarded numerous subjects because they were farm-related. When he was almost ready to give up in defeat, Lessy spoke.

"You know, the funniest thing happened to me today," she began.

"What?" he asked.

Lessy shrugged, a little unsure of herself. "Well, it's really ... I probably shouldn't even tell you this."

'Tell me," he insisted with a warm, open smile. "After a hard day's work a man needs a bit of humor come evening."

"Well, it was really quite embarrassing, actually," she said. "Sometimes our most embarrassing moments can really be very funny."

Vass chuckled with agreement, remembering some of his own. "I can't imagine what you could ever be embarrassed about," he said. "But I'm sitting with my ears perked, waiting to hear."

Lessy smiled a little shyly before giving a big sigh of resignation. "You know that tune you hum all the time?"

"Tune?"

"You know, the tune you hum while you're working."

"I hum?" He looked at her quizzically. "I didn't realize it."

"Yes, you are always humming this tune. I swear, every time I get near you or we're working together, you start humming this tune. I've come to think of it as sort of a part of you."

Vass was still smiling but shrugged in disbelief. "I can't imagine what it is."

"It goes—" Lessy hummed a few bars. Her rendition was a little off key, and Vass listened intently before he shook his head without recognition.

"Well, it's called—" She hesitated and then swallowed a giggling blush. "It's called 'Plowing Millie.' And I was humming it in the barn, not knowing what it was about. And that Mr. Ripley came in and started singing it. I declare, I must have turned every shade of red in the sunset."

Her words had run together rather quickly, but as she spoke, Vassar's eyes widened in shock and his jaw dropped open far enough to drive a team through.

In memory he saw himself, his older brothers, and their friends sitting behind the corncrib back at his daddy's farm. They were drinking root beer and pretending it was the real thing. Between swapping stories and speculation about women's anatomy, they sang the raunchy beer tunes of hardened rounders.

Sweet Millie whined
Now please be kind.
I almost am a virgin.
Except for Joe and Cousin Moe

And the baseball team at Spurgeon.

"RIPLEY SANG THAT SONG TO YOU!" THE WORDS came roaring out of Vassar's mouth with such fury that Lessy jumped.

"He sang the chorus, Vassar, only the chorus," Lessy insisted quickly. "He said that the verses weren't proper for me to hear."

"Nothing about that song is proper for *you* to hear."

Vass had risen angrily to his feet, and his hands were clenched in suppressed rage.

"It was my fault," Lessy insisted. "I was the one that was humming the song after all."

Vass turned to look at her, his eyes wild. "It was not *your* fault," he told her, keeping his voice deliberately controlled. "You would never think of doing anything shady or wicked."

Vassar was perfectly clear about whose fault it was. It was his own. What evil demon in his soul had him humming whoring ballads in the presence of a lady! *Be sure your sins will find you out* was more of a promise than a threat. Every day, every day, he tried to be worthy of Lessy, to be worthy of the woman of his dreams. But still he couldn't manage to live up to the man she believed him to be. He couldn't live up to the man that she deserved. His past sin might be forgiven, but the wickedness that still haunted his thoughts and his nights was not so easily vanquished.

"I need to take a walk," he announced as he moved toward the door.

Lessy hurried after him. "You're not going to do anything to Mr. Ripley?"

Vass looked back, surprised. "No, no, of course not." She was such a darling. Concerned for him, concerned for Ripley, never a thought to the terrible misdeed he had done, exposing her to the lowness of his own weakness. Vass reached over and patted her shoulder comfortingly. "I just need to be alone a while."

PULLING HIS HAT FROM HIS HEAD, VASS REACHED up to wipe the sweat from his brow. The teams had stopped moving, and the men had moved to the shady side of the horses as Lessy made her way through the group with cool water fresh from the well.

Beside him, Roscoe Doobervale spit a wad of tobacco into the new-mown field. "Don't like the looks of those clouds to the west," he said. "That's more than a chance shower, I'd stake my best boots on it."

Vass glanced in the direction he'd indicated and

nodded his head. "I suspect we'd best get what we can into the barn and let the rest meet the rain."

He didn't hear the old man's reply as his attention was drawn to the end of the wagon. Lessy and Ripley stood together, talking and laughing as if it were the easiest thing in the world. Rip was looking down into her eyes, his smile wide and his expression flirty. Lessy was looking back at him with only the palest flush of modesty on her face. What she told him made Ripley laugh, a deep hearty baritone, and she joined in with a tinkly giggle.

Watching them, there was little doubt in Vassar's mind that they had found something other than farming to talk about.

"Hey, Miss Lessy," Biggs called out. "Did you bring all that water for Ripley, or can the rest of us have some?"

Momentarily startled, Lessy looked at the water bucket in her hand as if she'd forgotten its existence. Then she gave Rip a feigned look of censure and shook her finger at him threateningly. "That's why you're trying to sweet-talk me! You want to keep this water within easy reach."

Ripley hung his head and placed his arms before her, wrists crossed like a guilty criminal asking to be led away. Lessy shook her head as she moved away, offering water to the rest of the men.

Vass valiantly attempted to focus his attention on what Doobervale was saying, but his eyes kept drifting to Lessy, whose cheeks were pink.

True to his word, he hadn't spoken to Ripley about the song. It was not Rip's fault, he'd concluded. It was surely his own. In the long night as he'd walked the peach orchard, he'd mentally cataloged his long list of sins.

He had wanted Lessy even before he'd ever seen her.

"It's no shame to have desire, son," his father had told him that long-ago summer. "But there is a place for it, and that place is the marriage bed."

Vass had hung his head in shame before his father. Shame had become his most familiar emotion. Shame was how he felt, and shame was what he'd brought, on his family and others.

"It just happened," he'd confessed to his father. "I don't know how it happened, it just did."

What had happened was Mrs. Mabel Brightmore. The wife of an aged and somewhat stodgy husband who was the local Granger representative. Mr. Brightmore was out of town quite frequently on business, and he'd hired Vass, then only seventeen, to take care of the heavy chores.

Those heavy chores had turned out to be more burdensome than he'd ever imagined. That long, blissful summer of his seventeenth year had been a sensual feast for a young man nearly starved. Mabel was enraptured with the broad young shoulders and the blushing innocence of the neighbor's boy.

"You don't know how lucky you are," she'd told him more than once as they lay in the lazy afterglow of an afternoon's illicit pleasures. "Why, your brothers and all your friends would just be green jealous if they knew that you and me were having such a good time."

He had felt lucky. He was hot and eager, randy and lucky. After a taste of the forbidden, he hadn't been willing to go back to being just another farmboy. It no longer mattered if Mr. Brightmore was due home any minute; they loitered in his bed illicitly. And if he were in the field, they could linger in the hayloft. And while the quiet, honest man spoke to his neighbors of farming concerns, Mabel and Vassar whispered coarse and wicked words in the seclusion of the Brightmore buggy or the broad daylight of Shady Creek bridge.

And Vass had thought himself the luckiest man on earth. Then his luck ran out.

"Harlot! Jezebel!" Vass could still hear Mr. Brightmore screaming through his tears. He'd surprised the two of them behind the men's privy at the Granger Hall. Nearly every man, woman, and child in Arkadelphia had been there. They'd heard

Brightmore's words, they'd stared at Mabel's disheveled clothes, and they'd witnessed Vassar's shame.

It was only his father and Reverend Watson who had kept old Brightmore from killing Vassar where he stood. There had been times when Vass had wished he had. Mabel left the county in disgrace. His parents could hardly hold their heads up in town. They decided to send him away.

"Hard work and your cousin Nora's moral values will keep you on the straight and narrow," his father had prophesied. "The only young woman within miles is little Lessy. And she is the kind you marry, not the kind you lust after."

But lust after her he had. She'd smiled her sweet innocent smile, and he'd gone as hot and hard as if Miss Mabel had run a long fingernail up his thigh.

Lessy was the kind of woman a man married, his father had said so. Even Vass could see the truth of that. Marriage was the perfect idea, he'd thought at first.

"That Lessy sure looks like Grandma Rooker," his father said to him that first day.

Vass had studied her face. He remembered his greatgrandmother only vaguely and could see nothing of the withered visage he remembered in the young, smooth cheeks before him. Still, Pa had said that it was so. And he found it disconcerting to imagine desire and lust with a ringer for Grandma Rooker.

So every time he looked at her, he thought of Grandma Rooker so he could keep his thoughts pure. And he'd managed to mend his ways.

Within a year he knew that to have a saint like Lessy for a wife would be more than any man could ask of heaven. But his dreams were still filled with sinful thoughts ...

Lessy was standing in front of him now, offering a dipper of cool water and looking at him curiously.

"What on earth are you thinking about, Vassar?" she asked. "I'll swan, you look to have your mind half across the globe."

He took the dipper and drank it down. "Looks like it's going to rain," he said with a gesture toward the western sky.

Lessy turned to look in that direction, raising a hand to her brow to shade the afternoon sun from her eyes.

"How far away is it?" she asked.

Vass had allowed his eyes to drop to the curve of her bosom and then mentally cursed himself for his weakness. He brought his gaze to her face to find her looking at him.

"What?" he asked with a nervous cough.

"The rain. How far away is the rain?"

"Oh! Late this evening or tonight, I suppose," he said. "I hope it clears up by morning. I'd hate to lose more than a day."

Suddenly Ripley was there, his arm slung casually around Lessy's waist, his voice loud and teasing. "You hear that, honey," he said. "Your bridegroom is so anxious to tie the knot, he's wishing the rain away. Never heard tell of a farmer doing that in all my days."

"Plenty do it in a flood," Doobervale piped in.

Rip gave a little moue of agreement and nodded his head. "A flood, you are right about that. And what we've got here is a flood of love."

The crew chuckled at his words, clearly enjoying the joke on the young couple.

Lessy laughed also as she elbowed Ripley playfully. "You are the biggest sack of foolishness God ever put into the body of a man."

Rip grinned at her. "And what does a sweet little farm girl like you know about men's bodies?"

Lessy's hand flew to her mouth in shock. Vass felt his whole muscles going tense, and his jaw set dangerously.

"Whoops," Rip said quietly as he caught sight of Vassar's expression. With exaggerated motions he withdrew his arm from Lessy's waist and stepped back with his hands up in a gesture of surrender. "Just teasing, Mr. Muldrow, sir. What's a wedding without a little good-natured teasing?"

The humorous murmurs from the other men seemed to be in agreement, so Vass let his anger go.

Although not completely. A part of him continued to simmer that Ripley had made suggestive remarks to Lessy.

And that she hadn't fainted away in shock and horror.

CHAPTER 5

The rain had arrived just after darkness fell, but it had not dissipated with the dawn. Dismal gray clouds hung overhead, and a slow steady shower rained down on the farm.

Lessy slogged through her chores with less enthusiasm than usual. Vass had been avoiding her since their talk in the parlor, and she feared that he thought the worst of her. She knew Vass to be a very moral, very upright gentleman. He must be horrified by her commonness.

Sugie Jo had once complained bitterly about how men— all men, young and old, rich or poor, farmer or tradesman—turned into twelve-handed boars in rut when they found themselves alone with a woman. Lessy was sure that Sugie Jo exaggerated, as was her nature, but even Mammy said a fellow was likely to try to steal a kiss.

Vassar, however, had never so much as made an improper suggestion.

And she was beginning to suspect why.

Vass, her Vass, had hummed a naughty ditty as he worked beside her. It seemed that Vassar perhaps wasn't the stalwart young man she thought him to be. Perhaps it wasn't his high moral nature that kept him at a distance from her. Perhaps it was something lacking in herself. When he was alone with her, he thought about farming. If he were to be alone with Sugie Jo, would his thoughts be different?

"All work and no play makes the bride look tired on her wedding day!"

Lessy started at the unexpected voice and turned in the direction of the caller. She spied Ripley seated underneath the tarp that the men had raised over their little camp. A light glowed from a lantern beside him, highlighting his face.

With a wave of his arm he called her over.

She walked closer, within easy speaking distance but still far from the tarp. "I can't come in there," she protested.

Rip gave her a look of long-suffering patience. "Now, Miss Lessy," he said with light sarcasm. "It is broad daylight, and anybody within a half mile of the farmhouse can see us plainly. Come on inside and get out of the rain. I've got something to show you."

Lessy hesitated a minute more and then shrugged. Rip was absolutely right. The tarp may be where the men slept, but on a day like this it was hardly a private assignation. She stepped beneath the cover of the tent and pulled the sodden rain bonnet from her hair.

"Where are the rest of the men?" she asked.

Rip shrugged. "In the barn, I suppose, cleaning harness."

Lessy nodded. It seemed a likely occupation on such a day. "Why aren't you helping?"

"I will if they ask me," he said. "But if they don't notice that I'm not there, I'm not about to point it out."

"You'd rather sit out here and do nothing?" Her expression was incredulous.

"I'm doing something."

"What are you doing?"

"Drawing."

"Drawing? Pictures? Oh, let me see!" There was enthusiasm in her voice as she hurriedly seated herself beside him.

Rip seemed amused at her excitement and a little apologetically handed her the paper he was working on. Lessy stared at it curiously. The pen and ink drawing was all circles and perfectly straight lines. She couldn't quite make out what it was supposed to be. Biting her lip nervously and glancing at him under lowered lids, she turned the picture upside down, hoping the image would reveal itself. It did not.

"It's lovely," she said politely.

Rip laughed out loud and leaned over to squeeze her shoulders. "Lovely? Well, ma'am, you must really have farming in your blood to see a side-loading packer binder and think it lovely."

"A side-loading packer binder?"

Her expression was so dumbstruck, Rip squeezed her shoulders again. "Yes, Miss Lovely Lessy. This is my latest design. I've been working on it all summer. Hope by fall to sell it to one of the farm implement companies, McCormick or Ralston maybe."

"You design farm implements?"

Rip nodded. "Indeed I do." He pulled a tablet wrapped in sealskin from his grip. "I've designed machines that will do everything on a farm but kiss the babies."

"Let me see."

He did, showing her page after page of neat, intricate mechanical drawings.

"If what you really do is design farm equipment, why are you working on a hay crew?"

Rip shrugged. "I *design* equipment," he said. "You only make money if you *sell* your designs."

"But you said McCormick or Ralston—"

Rip shook his head. "I'm dreaming," he admitted. "They have more engineers and draftsmen in those companies than ticks on a blue hound. They aren't very likely to buy something from outside when they can get it from their own people for free."

"But you keep trying."

"Can't stop," he said. "Once you start a thing, it kind of gets in your blood and you can't get away from it. It doesn't seem to matter what the truth is or if it's the right thing to do. Once you've invested a goodly amount of time on something, it seems you just can't quit it. It's funny really."

Lessy didn't think it was a bit funny. That was exactly what she had done with Vass. She'd decided that she wanted to marry him, and she'd pursued him obstinately. Now she was only weeks away from the wedding, and she was wondering if their perfect matchup was full of corn borers.

"If I had a lick of sense," Rip was saying, "I'd quit this nonsense and find me a real job."

"No, not that," Lessy told him. "If you had a lick of sense you'd go into business for yourself."

Rip laughed humorlessly. "Me and whose bank?"

"You don't need a bank, you just need some farmers with a little money to invest. And there is no better place to find those than right here. We've had three good harvests in a row. Folks here about are looking for a good place to put what's stuffed in the mattress."

"Nobody around here even knows me."

'They don't have to know you, just your designs. I'm no engineer, but some of the farmers around here know a lot about equipment. If it's really good, they'll be able to tell."

Ripley shrugged, not quite dismissing her idea.

"I can see it now," she said. "Rip Ripley Farm Machinery." She hesitated. "No, that will never do. What is your given name?"

"My given name?"

"Your given name. John Ripley, Will Ripley, Chester Ripley?"

He shook his head. "Just Ripley, ma'am. My name is such an embarrassment, I don't even remember it anymore."

Lessy nodded. "All right. Then Ripley and Sons —that sounds very official, don't you think? The kind of long term solid company a farmer can trust."

"I have no sons."

She waved away his concern. "Believe me, when

you own your own manufacturing company, some woman will marry you up real fast."

"They might try."

Lessy laughed. "Oh, a confirmed bachelor. I suppose you know that women love a challenge."

His expression was careless and his shrug teasing. "Seriously, though," she said, "I believe that we should all try to find a way to achieve our heart's desire. It is such a waste of our gifts if we don't."

Ripley's expression became solemn. "I'm going to do it someday. I just have to wait for the right time, settle down, and get started."

"I could ask Vassar to have a look at your drawings, if you like," she said. "I'm sure he has money to invest." Her sincerity and determination showed clearly on her face, and the sight brought a warm tenderness to Ripley's smile. He brought a hand to her cheek and smoothed away a damp tendril of hair that clung there.

"You are really a fine kind of woman, Lessy. You are surely what God had in mind when he used the word *helpmate.*"

Lessy's eyes widened, and she shook her head in disagreement. "No, I'm not really like that," she confessed. "I pretend to be that way, but I'm really just foolish and selfish."

Rip's expression turned quizzical. "What a strange thing to say."

Lessy blushed. "It's true," she said quietly. Suddenly she wanted somebody to know the truth. "I'm really not as hardworking and temperate as I seem."

"You're not?" Ripley clearly did not believe her, but was intrigued by the possibility.

"I. .. well, I started acting that way for Vass."

Raising an eyebrow, he looked at her curiously. "Vass wants you to act hardworking and temperate?"

"Oh, no. I mean yes." She was both confused and embarrassed at her own revelation. "Well, he doesn't know that it's an act. He thinks I really *am* the person I've been pretending to be."

Rip leaned closer, resting his hand on his chin. "And why have you been pretending to be some other person, Miss Lessy?"

"I'm not exactly pretending to be another person. I'm just... well, I'm trying to be the woman that Vass would want to marry." She lowered her head shamefully. "I can't believe I've told this to you. It's really terrible, isn't it?"

She looked up to find Rip grinning ear to ear. "Yes, Lessy, it is very terrible, a sin of major proportions to allow your intended to think the best of you. But, truth to tell, I've never met a woman —or a man, either—that was exactly what he seemed to be before the wedding."

"Well," Lessy admitted, "maybe most folks are on their best behavior before the wedding, but I'm just an out- and-out liar. Vass doesn't know that I have a temper or that I daydream during Sunday School or that I only like gardening because it gives me an excuse to dig around in the dirt like a gopher."

Rip smiled at her. "I doubt the man will care. When a fellow's in love, he can forgive a lot in a woman."

"What if he's not in love?" Lessy's words were only a whisper.

Rip took her chin in his hand and raised her eyes to his. "None of that nonsense," he said. "Vassar Muldrow is so much in love, he looks like a mule hit between the eyes with a poleax."

She was doubtful, but she didn't want to confess the rest. "But he's in love with someone I've pretended to be."

Rip shook his head. "He's in love with you, Lessy Green. Believe me, when that man is kissing your sweet lips, the last thing he's thinking about is what occupies your mind during Sunday School."

That was the problem, Lessy thought with despair. He didn't seem to want to kiss her.

The rain finally stopped late in the day, and the sun came out with blistering ferocity. Steam rose from the ground in eerie little patches, and the men were as wet from sweat as if they were still working in the rain.

Because dinner was early and the day had been a slow one, it was expected that Vass and Lessy would walk out after supper. Both knew that it would appear strange if they did not. But both would have forgone the experience if they'd been offered the chance.

Vass rose from the table and offered Lessy his arm in a most gentlemanly fashion. This action drew a tableful of catcalls, and the two embarrassed young people could not get away from the group quickly enough. They walked in silence as far as the peach orchard, when the strain became too much for Lessy.

"I'm sorry about the song," she said. She didn't look at him, and unable to gauge his reaction, she blundered on. "It was the kind of distressing moment that a woman should have just forced herself to immediately forget. I should never have passed on the incident like a careless piece of gossip."

"It was all my fault, Lessy, and I do beg your forgiveness. But please let us not talk about it anymore."

Lessy nodded agreeably as she mentally berated herself for once again bringing the subject up. Talking so openly and easily with Rip had loosened her guard. She had to remind herself how Vass preferred women who were more upstanding.

Conversation waned as Vass was loath to bring up the farm for discussion and Lessy was second-guessing every thought that came to mind.

"Did you know that Mr. Ripley does mechanical drawing?" she asked finally.

Vass looked at her curiously. In memory he could see the two of them with their heads together giggling like children. It was an incongruous image, but one that had him stinging with jealousy. "No, I was not aware of that," he said.

"Well, I saw some of his drawings today, and I really think that you should have a look at them."

"Really?"

With the natural confusion of the nonmechanically minded, Lessy explained the side-loading packer binder, the double row corn planter, and the other implements that she had seen. Vass listened with some interest as he watched the enthusiastic expression on Lessy's face. Was she enthusiastic about the machines or about the man?

"He's really quite talented, and I thought you might look at his work and give him your opinion."

Vass nodded. "Well, certainly I would. Roscoe said that he was very handy with the equipment, but I never would have guessed he had ideas for machines of his own."

Lessy smiled. "He says the implement companies are not interested in inventions from outsiders. But I think he could go into business for himself if his ideas were sound and he had some farmer investors to back him."

"It's certainly possible," Vass said, slightly surprised by her enthusiasm. He'd never doubted that Lessy had a keen mind; she always agreed with him. But she'd never come up with ideas of her own.

"You like Ripley, don't you?" His question was somewhat abrupt.

Lessy was momentarily taken aback. "Well, yes, of course I like him. He's a very entertaining man. He tells such funny stories, I swan, he has me laughing all the time."

Vass wondered if he himself ever made her laugh. At that moment he couldn't remember a single time.

"The fellows tell me he's very popular with women," Vass said tentatively.

Lessy grinned. "I'm sure that he is. My lands, the things he says! He must be breaking hearts all across Arkansas."

Because she said it with good humor, Vass didn't tell her that her little joke was very likely true.

"I didn't see Rip in the bam today. Where did you talk to him?"

Lessy couldn't meet Vassar's eyes. "Under the tarp," she said a little too hurriedly. "We were just sitting under the tarp to be out of the rain."

Having been beneath that tarp on several occasions, a mental image flashed through Vassar's brain of an eight by ten foot space that was a long row of bedrolls—men's bedrolls. The color drained from his face.

"We were just getting out of the rain," Lessy said again.

His thoughts whirling in confusion, Vass imagined that he saw Lessy, his Lessy, laying back on a tattered bedroll that smelled of men. Her eyes were not trusting and innocent, but earthy and eager. And he saw himself kneeling down before her. In his mind he clutched the hem of her calico work dress and raised it to her waist with indecent haste.

He quickly tried to think of Grandma Rooker. But this time the old trick didn't work.

"Nothing happened!" Lessy's nervous insistence finally brought Vass back to reality.

"Of course not, Lessy," he assured her, although he gripped her hand a bit tightly. "With a woman like you, I know that nothing untoward would happen."

Lessy hesitated a moment before responding with a tentative thank-you.

They continued their walk silently in the direction of the pond. Vass kept his eyes straight ahead, trying not to think of Lessy in sinful ways. Although it was hard since she was right beside him, smelling of soap and starch.

Lessy's mind was also in turmoil. Did he trust her so completely because he believed her to be so virtuous or because he saw her as so undesirable?

In the growing darkness near the pond, neither saw the puddled evidence of the day's rain until Lessy slipped in the mud. Her boot slid out from beneath her, and she was headed for an indecorous splat on the soggy ground.

"Oh!"

Her cry was hardly out of her mouth before Vassar was there. He more than caught her—he wrapped his arms around her and whisked her out of the mud, lifting her against his chest.

For Lessy the moment was almost heart-stopping. The startled surprise of a near splash in a mud puddle was immediately followed by this evidence of masculine strength as the man after her own heart held her closely against his.

Vass stepped back and held her only a moment longer than necessary. The welcome weight of the woman in his arms nearly stunned him brain-numb. He wanted to bury his face in the cool softness of her throat, taste her lips, and explore her with his tongue. He wanted to send his hands a-roving the sensuous hills and valleys of the woman in his arms. He did none of these.

"I'm sorry, Lessy, I led you right into the mud," he said as he stood her upright on what seemed to Lessy to be very shaky solid firmament.

Her feet touched the ground, and he dropped his arms from her. But Lessy did not move away.

"Vass?" Her voice was only a whisper.

He looked at her face only inches from his own and swallowed nervously.

"Vass?" she whispered again.

"Lessy." Her name came out a gravelly plea.

"Kiss me."

"Lessy."

"Kiss me."

He swallowed. His heart was pounding like an infantry drum during full frontal attack. The scent and warmth of her skin still clung to his shirtfront. His hands trembled with desire. Kiss her? Oh, yes, he would kiss her. He would kiss her and hold her and pull her to the ground, right here in the mud, and make her his, truly his, as he had always wanted.

Painfully he set his jaw against his inclination and forced himself to step back.

His retreat stabbed Lessy like a wound, and tears stung her eyes.

"Don't you want to kiss me?"

"Of course I do," he insisted. His voice was still a little shaky, and he wiped his sweating palms against his trousers before he placed his hands gently on her shoulders. Leaning down he brushed her lips as lightly as he had before. It was the way Lessy might have kissed her mother. Even Lessy's inexperience in such matters could not hide from her that his was not a lover's kiss.

"We'd best go back to the house," he said.

Lessy nodded, her heart in her throat. With a kiss like that she was sure a man might easily be thinking about what occupied her thoughts during Sunday School.

CHAPTER 6

"Yoohoo! Yoohoo!"

Lessy was pouring the last cup of breakfast coffee around the table when the rattle of a rig on the drive captured her attention only an instant before she heard the call.

"Yoohoo! Lessy!"

Rip looked up from a conversation with Angus, his glance furrowing to incredulity.

"Who is that?"

Lessy waved her arm broadly in greeting.

Dressed in a bright pink gingham that was cut much too form-fitting for farm work, Sugie Jo Mouwers bounced excitedly on the wagon seat, her blond curls fluttering in the breeze as she waved a dainty pink handkerchief.

Beside the pretty young woman, Joseph Mouwers sat stem and stoic as was his nature, making it difficult for all to imagine how such a straight and narrow worker ant, solemnly doing his duty, could have ever fathered such a frivolous butterfly as Sugie Jo.

"Morning, Mr. Mouwers." Vass offered the greeting as the wagon pulled up before the house. "Morning, Miss Sugie Jo."

"Is it true? Is it finally true?" Sugie Jo's questions were high-pitched with excitement and aimed at both Vass and Lessy. Not waiting for an answer, she scrambled down from the wagon with only minimal assistance from Vass to wrap her arms eagerly around Lessy. 'Tell me! I couldn't wait another day to hear it for myself. Are you and Vass really getting married?"

Lessy blushed and gave Vass a shy glance before nodding affirmatively.

"Yeeeek!" Sugie Jo began jumping up and down, her arms around Lessy, taking her along. "I'm so excited! It finally happened! I knew it would. I just knew it."

Joseph Mouwers managed to ignore his daughter's girlish glee as if he were both deaf and blind. "Figured after that storm you all wouldn't be in the fields today," he said to Vass with a nod to Roscoe coming up beside him. "Suspect you'll be checking harness and sharpening implements today."

Vassar nodded.

"With all these men drawing wages," Mouwers said with a disapproving gesture at the men still seated at the breakfast table, "I thought you might as well work on mine, too." He indicated the plow blade he carried in his wagon and the disk harrow that trailed behind. "If you are bringing your crew to my place next, I don't want you getting used to loafing away your time."

Doobervale bristled.

Joseph Mouwers had a way of bringing out the devil in the best of Christians. Vass was used to stepping in to smooth things over.

With familiarity that made for unconcern, Sugie Jo pulled Lessy away from the men. "I want to hear everything!" she declared dramatically. "Don't even keep the most private of details from me!"

Lessy smiled and shook her head at her exuberant friend. "Sugie Jo, there really isn't that much to tell."

"I don't believe a word of it! I want the whole truth. Was the moon full? Did he go down on one knee? Did you say yes right away or leave him dangling a week or two?"

Lessy giggled at the ridiculousness of the idea.

From the comer of her eye she spotted Rip and immediately motioned for him to come over.

"I want you to meet this really sweet fellow that's come with the haying crew," Lessy said as Rip walked toward them. "I know you two are just going to like each other immediately."

Sugie Jo looked up, but her expression darkened. By the time Rip stood at their side, his face was a mask of disapproval and his mouth was drawn into one thin line.

"Sugie Jo, this is Rip Ripley. He works on Mr. Doobervale's crew, and he designs the most impressive- looking farm machines you ever saw." Lessy turned back to Rip. "This is Sugie Jo Mouwers. She and her family are our closest neighbors, and we've been friends since we fit in the same laundry basket."

Lessy's smile was wide with pleasure at the introduction but faltered slightly at the curt nods of acknowledgment her friends exchanged.

"Miss Mouwers."

"Mr. Ripley."

Rip's smile was reserved for Lessy as he took his leave, professing an urgent desire to help the other men. Surprised, Lessy turned to her friend in question.

"Do you two know each other?"

Sugie Jo shook her head. "No, I don't know him. But I know his type."

"His type?"

The pretty blonde nodded, her curls bouncing affirmatively. "He's one of those sweet-talking heartbreakers," she said. "As pretty as a baby skunk and a whole lot more dangerous. You'd best stay away from that one, Lessy. He's nothing but trouble."

Lessy's mouth dropped open in surprise. "He seems like a perfectly nice young man to me."

Sugie Jo nodded sagely. "I'm sure that Eve thought the serpent to be just a friendly lizard, too."

Later as the two picked beans in the garden, Lessy told about her engagement.

"So it's really not going to be that big of a change," she said with an air of feigned maturity. "We'll just go on living the lives we've always lived."

Sugie Jo didn't giggle at that—she laughed out loud. "Lessy Green, I swear you've got no more sense of things than a rabbit." She stopped to pull off the bright pink bonnet and shake her curls in the barest of morning breezes. "Here you are just weeks away from doing the *big naughty* with the fellow you've been pining after for four years. And you talk as if it's of no more importance than switching Sunday School classes."

Lessy raised her chin defiantly. "I think all the stories we've heard about this man-woman thing are just made up. I think it's not really so much."

"Well, you're wrong," Sugie Jo insisted. "The *big naughty* is even bigger than we ever thought."

Lessy was skeptical. "It's just nature, like growing up or having a baby. All those things they say about getting weak-kneed and falling off the edge of the world, that's just talk."

"It's not just talk," her friend insisted.

"How would you know? I'm the one that's betrothed."

Sugie Jo raised an eyebrow loftily. "I guess you've forgot that *I* was engaged to Homer Deathridge all last winter."

Staring at her friend for a long moment, the import of Sugie Jo's words finally soaked in and Lessy squealed in scandal-shocked delight as she leapt across a half dozen rows of snap beans to grasp her friend around the waist.

"You did the big naughty with Homer Deathridge?" Lessy's whisper was half awe—half horror.

"Not the whole thing," Sugie Jo assured her with a nervous glance around to assure herself there was no one within earshot.

"How much?"

Sugie Jo hesitated. "I let him touch me."

"On your bosom?"

"Oh, for heaven's sake," Sugie Jo complained, shaking her pretty blond curls with disbelief. "You can't even get engaged without letting them touch you there! No, silly goose, I let him really touch me, touch me down there."

Her eyes widening with shock, Lessy gave an involuntary glance toward Sugie Jo's skirts.

"Down there?"

"Through my clothes, of course."

"Of course!"

A hushed, uncomfortable silence fell between them. Lessy swallowed nervously.

"So how did it feel?" she asked finally.

Again Sugie Jo hesitated, as if wavering about her admission. "*Wonderful.*" The word exploded from her, and Sugie Jo blushed furiously before covering her mouth with her hand and emitting an earsplitting screech.

The two young women clasped hands in giggling glee.

"You just wait," Sugie Jo promised. "When Vassar lays his hands on you, you are going to think you've died and gone to glory."

Lessy hugged her tightly, trying to hold in the thrill and anxiety and fear that curled up inside her.

"If it was so wonderful," she asked finally, "why did you break off with Homer?"

Sugie Jo shrugged. "Oh, I'm not silly enough to think that Homer's the only fellow who could make me feel that way. And I think Daddy liked him better than I did. That, in itself, is enough to worry a gal into breaking it off."

It was near noontime before Joseph Mouwers had his blades all honed to his liking. He flatly refused an invitation to luncheon, stating tactlessly that the Widow Green's cooking never set well on his stomach.

"I hope I see you again before the wedding," Sugie Jo told Lessy as they parted. "'Cause I'm sure I won't see much of you afterward. I bet that Vassar keeps you within hugging reach from then on."

Lessy smiled with delight at the prospect, but reality couldn't quite be ignored. As she watched the Mouwerses driving away, Sugie Jo bouncing up and down on the seat, her father staring straight at the horses in front of him as if he were completely alone, Lessy couldn't help but worry. Would Vassar ever want to touch her? And if he did, would she really think that she'd died and gone to glory? Or was that special feeling only for pretty girls like Sugie Jo?

. . .

"COME HELP ME PICK PEACHES." LESSY'S WORDS were more in the nature of a command than a request, and Rip immediately discarded the gearing box design he was working on to follow her.

The sun was shining brightly this afternoon, making it hot and muggy, but all were hopeful that by tomorrow the fields would be dry enough for haying.

Lessy had been uncharacteristically quiet both at breakfast and the noon meal. Even now her thoughts appeared to be elsewhere as she made her way to the orchard, an empty bushel basket hanging from her left hand.

Ripley had to hurry to catch up with her, and when he took the basket, her smile of thanks seemed more sad than grateful.

"Not many peaches left," he said conversationally as they walked through the neat rows of tall, well-tended trees.

"It's late in the year," she agreed. "But I never let a peach go to waste." She spied a bright yellow fruit with a rusty red blush on its cheek and reached up on her tiptoes to pull it down. "It really takes more time to pick what's left than when the trees are full, because you have to move the ladder with you constantly."

Taking her words as a suggestion, Rip retrieved the folding ladder that leaned against a nearby tree trunk and began following Lessy with it in hand. They stopped at first one tree and then the next as she climbed up the ladder to reach the higher limbs that held a few stray ripe peaches.

Her thoughtful expression caused worry lines to form on her brow.

"This is a mighty fine orchard, Miss Lessy," Rip told her, trying to lighten her mood.

Lessy smiled gently, her voice a soft whisper. "My grandmother planted it. When I was young, I thought of it as my own secret hideaway where everything that I ever wanted would always come true." Suddenly recalling herself, she cast off the hint of dreaminess in her expression. "Vass said pecans would have been better."

Rip's expression was puzzled as he raised an eyebrow in disagreement. "I like peaches."

"Me, too," Lessy agreed as she climbed up the ladder. "There is nothing better than fresh peach cobbler. But Vass is right, pecans would have been more practical."

Rip held the ladder steady as she reached a high and heavy branch. Lessy could feel the heat of his gaze upon her. The strangeness of the feeling caused her to speak more rapidly than she would have.

"Pecans are easier to grow," she said. "And they keep much better than peaches, even when they are in preserves. And when there's a need to cull the trees, the wood of the pecan is valuable in itself. Peachwood is good for nothing."

"I don't know about that," Rip said with a smile. "My mama used to make some mighty fine switches from the tree in our yard."

Lessy giggled at his comical expression of remembered pain as she gently placed another bright, blushing peach in the basket. "With pecans you're free of the time spent handpicking. You can simply shake the nuts down from the trees without a worry about breaking or bruising them." Lessy nodded determinedly. "Pecans are definitely a more practical orchard tree."

Rip brought a handful of sweet-smelling ripe peaches and laid most of them carefully in the basket. One, the darkest, ripest, most perfect, he held out to her like the temptation in the Garden of Eden. "Practical should not be a woman's first concern," he said. "And what's most fine to have in this world is not always the easiest to get. Lots of the best things in life are clearly not practical." He waved the peach slowly under her nose. The sultry, sweet scent assailed her. "Music and dancing and laughing aren't what you'd call practical, but life wouldn't be nearly so happy without them."

"Well, certainly we wouldn't want to give up our humanity for practicality," she said, grabbing the peach from him, unable to resist taking a large greedy bite. It was sweet and juicy, and Lessy's tongue darted out to capture the juice that threatened to drip down her chin. "But pecans over peaches seems a very small compromise to make."

Rip came to stand in front of her, holding the ladder between them. "It's the little compromises like that, Miss Lessy, that will take all the sweetness out of a life." Lessy let his words pass, hastily dropping her gaze and moving along to the next tree. But as they continued their way through the cooling shade of peach boughs, her mind dwelled upon them.

Stopping, she took another bite from the peach he'd given her, tasting the sweet, sticky smoothness that could never be supplanted by the finest-tasting pecans. "Ripley," she asked, as if she could no longer keep her silence, "how important is it to a man that his wife be pretty?"

The young man was a bit startled by the question. She was unwilling to look at him directly, which gave him opportunity to observe her discomfiture. "You thinking of your friend, Miss Mouwers?"

"Oh, no," Lessy insisted. "I was just asking. But you didn't like Sugie Jo."

"I liked her fine," he said. "What's not to like? She's a fine looker for sure."

Lessy was puzzled. "You didn't act like you liked her."

"Just being careful," he replied. "She's one fine looker who is a-looking to get married. So I don't want her looking in *my* direction."

"But she's very pretty."

Rip nodded in agreement.

"So how important is it to a man that his woman be pretty?"

Ripley turned to look at her. "For most men it's very important," he said at first and then hesitated as if thinking. "Well, I guess it's pretty important." Stopping completely, he shook his head, and with a light chuckle as he bent over to catch her downcast eyes he told her finally, "Maybe it ain't a bit important at all."

Lessy folded her arms across her chest stubbornly in disapproval. "Which is it?" she asked. "Very important, pretty important, or not important at all?"

Rip looked at the young woman with some curiosity and a good deal of cockiness as he leaned indolently against a tree trunk. "Miss Lessy," he said, "it's all three."

She raised an eyebrow.

'To find a woman, a man's got to notice her. If he passes by her in church without ever speaking, it ain't likely they'll ever be together. But if she's a fine looker, say like your friend, Miss Mouwers," he said, "then it's not likely he'll pass by without seeing her."

Lessy nodded. "So it's very important that she be pretty."

Rip shook his head. "Now, most of us fellows meet a gal through family or friends, and usually you get to know her a bit before you'd ever think of walking out with her. If she's pleasant and sweet, you're interested whether she's eye-popping or no. But still, when a man's got that gal on his arm, he wants her to be looking good. He wants the other fellows to be green with envy. That makes a fellow feel pretty cocky. But a man won't bother to sashay around with a woman he don't cotton to."

"So it's pretty important," Lessy said.

Rip reached out a hand and raised Lessy's chin. He looked into her eyes. She was no beauty, but there was strength and substance to her that held a lure all its own. His smile was warm and bright. "When it comes to walking out, yes. But you said *wife,* Miss Lessy. In a wife it ain't important at all."

Lessy's eyes widened with surprise.

"Us country boys may act the fool," Ripley told her. "But most of us are smart enough to know that a pretty child at sixteen may not be worth her weight in beans as a helpmate at forty-five. It's what's inside a woman that makes you choose her for a wife. Her heart, her soul, her dreams ... that makes a man want to live a lifetime with her. If the feeling and yearnings all fit, it don't matter if the gal is belle of the county or fit to wear a cowbell."

His words scoured a rough tenderness in Lessy's heart, and she blinked back a burning in her eyes that she feared might be tears.

"But what if the man doesn't really know who she is inside? And what if he thinks the woman to be a good helpmate but can't bring himself to sweeten toward her? Could a man marry a woman that he has no ... no yearning for?"

The tears were welling, unwanted, in the comers of her eyes, and she tried to drop her gaze from Rip's expression that had been teasing and sweet but had now turned tender and concerned.

With a hint of anger in her motion, she cast the halfeaten peach in her hand into the distant grass. "I'm just being foolish—" she began, trying to turn away.

Rip did not let her. He slipped his arm around her waist and pulled her close to him. "Are you being foolish, Miss Lessy? Or is it that big farmer of yours who's a fool?"

Standing in his arms, Lessy looked up at the dark, handsome face above her, and she knew he was going to kiss her. He did not hold her tightly, and his hesitation was clearly to give her time to retreat. She did not.

His mouth touched hers with skill and confidence. He traced the line of her lips with his tongue, causing Lessy to startle.

Ripley grinned at her innocent surprise. "The sweetest peach in Arkansas," he whispered against her as he opened her mouth to get another taste.

"DADBURNIT!" ROSCOE SWORE. "THIS WAGON jack ain't worth throwing into the scrap heap."

The men around him were nodding their heads in agreement, but Vass only chuckled. "Now, you can't go blaming this poor hardworking little jack for not being able to do something that I told you would need a rope and pulley."

Doobervale threw up his hands in defeat. "Lord love you, Muldrow, I'm just grateful you ain't a betting man, or I'd a lost money on this one."

The empty hay wagon was bogged down in the mud on the low side of the barn. Young McFadden, in the ignorance of youth, had left it there when he'd driven it out of the field. Doobervale had insisted that a wagon jack would be enough to rescue it. He might have been right if they'd begun working at it early in the morning, as they'd planned. But after hours of tool sharpening, both their own and Mouwers's, the muddy ground had hardened, holding the wagon wheels to it like molasses turned into hard candy.

"Get me that rope and tackle that I left on the floor of the harness room." Vass directed the order to young Tommy, whose cheeks were still alternately pale and flushed with the humiliation of his mistake. "We can throw it over the ridge pole of the bam and get all the leverage we need." Vass looked up to the timber that extended out from the peak of the bam roof, wondering if there would be enough rope.

"With a whole crew of men this shouldn't be too much of a chore." Glancing around, a furrow came into his brow. "Where's Ripley?"

Doobervale shrugged with unconcern. "That one is the very best to have when a man's working with equipment. But he's got a real aversion to putting his back into a job." The men around him chuckled.

"Ripley," Claidon Biggs declared, "don't never lift nothing heavier than a petticoat if he can help it."

These words gained guffaws all around, and young McFadden, hoping to get himself back in with the boys, added his own little joke. "I know that's got to be true," the boy claimed. "Here we are sweating over a stuck wagon, and I spied him walking out into the shade of the peach trees with Miss Lessy."

The laughter the boy had hoped for fell a little flat as Vass gave him a sharp look. Without further comment Vassar hoisted the rope over the ridge pole and set up the pulley. He worked with certainty and efficiency born of habit, but his thoughts were elsewhere.

Lessy and Ripley alone in the peach orchard? It just didn't seem proper somehow. Lessy was so innocent and trusting. A man like Ripley might take advantage of her sweet nature. In his memory he could hear the two of them laughing together in the kitchen. And she was so enthusiastic about his drawings. They had been alone together under that camp tarp. Could that no-account rounder be whispering pretty words to his Lessy? Vass could hardly keep his feet in the spot. As soon as he assured himself that the knotting was secure, he handed the end ropes to Doobervale.

"I need to get a drink of water," he announced lamely. Walking away, Vass didn't dare to look back on the bewildered expressions of the men he'd left.

Making no pretense of even going near the house, he headed straight to the peach orchard. The thoughts in his mind spun in wild imagining, but he wouldn't focus on them. Lessy was in the orchard with Ripley, and he was merely going to join them. He was only going for a friendly chat. He was only going to ask Ripley to come help with the wagon.

LESSY BROKE AWAY FROM THE KISS AND STARED into Ripley's eyes. They were smoky and half-closed with such an expression of ardor that she giggled.

His mouth dropped open with surprise.

"Mr. Ripley," she said. "You look at me like I was a peach cobbler myself. And I'm practically an old married lady."

His surprise melting into delight, he leaned forward once more and teased her lips with his tongue. When she drew back, he winked broadly. "You aren't married yet, Miss Lessy. Ain't no sin in taking a last long look at freedom. I *am* from the haying crew, and they do say to make hay while the sun shines."

She laughed at his teasing and had actually raised her lips for more of his special brand of hay-making when over his shoulder she caught sight of a large, work-hardened blond man gazing at them in horror.

"Vassar!"

Ripley jumped away from her as if shot from a gun.

His face pale and pained, Vassar Muldrow paced slow, heavy steps toward them.

Lessy had never thought of Vass as a man of violence, but the expression on his face, normally so calm and controlled, was frightening in its intensity.

"Don't hit him, Vass!" Lessy said, bravely stepping in front of the handsome dark-haired man. "It's my fault, not his. I let him kiss me. I wanted him to."

Her words had the same effect on Vass as being kicked in the stomach by an ornery mule. He paled and sweat broke across his brow.

Ripley easily stepped around Lessy, his hands held high in a gesture of surrender. "You want to punch me, Muldrow?" he said. "Well, take your shot. But it was nothing more than a stolen kiss, and it was headed nowhere."

Vassar's face was now florid, and his breathing came in frightening puffs of anger, but his eyes, as he looked at the couple before him, were full of pain. He swallowed hard.

"Doobervale needs a hand at the barn," he said to Ripley, his tone brooking no question.

The young man glanced toward Lessy. "Are you going to be all right?" he asked her. "Are you safe with him?"

Before Lessy could nod her assurance, Vassar

exploded. "What kind of man do you take me for? She's been safe with me for years before she ever knew you existed!"

Lessy nodded to the young man to go. Vass stood, fists clenched until Rip had walked away. Then, with a sigh that seemed to wilt the steel in his backbone, Vassar took a step closer, leaning against the ladder as if he could no longer stand on his own power.

Hearing the pained gasp of his breath, Lessy watched him squeeze his eyes together as if to hold back the tide that threatened to pour from them. Her own eyes were now swimming with tears that she tried to wipe on her apron.

"I'm so sorry Vassar," she managed to choke out. "I have lied to you, so many lies, I'm not the woman that you think I am. I am lazy and frivolous, and I let a man kiss me just because I wanted him to. I've deceived you into believing that I am better than I am, but I never meant harm. Can you ever forgive me?"

It was as if Vassar had not heard her words. "Don't worry, Lessy," he said. "I should have seen this coming. I did see it—I just didn't want to believe it true. I'll see that he marries you up good and proper. I'm wise to his ways and reputation, and I won't have him leaving any broken hearts on this farm."

"What?"

"A fine woman like you is not to be dallied with and left behind. I'll see that he stands up to his responsibilities if it takes a shotgun to do it."

She gawked at him, swiping at her eyes distractedly. "Responsibilities?"

"He's not the kind of man I would have wanted for you, Lessy. But there ain't a man living that's half good enough to husband you. I guess he has no more faults than me."

"Vassar, what are you saying?"

"I won't stand in your way, Lessy. I know that you love him, and I care too much for you to hold you back."

"OH, MAMMY! WHAT AM I GOING TO DO?"

Lessy's tears dampened the cotton quilt that covered her bed, darkening the bright yellow and blue patterns of Sunbonnet Sue.

Rip had come to the porch right after dinner. She hadn't seen Vassar in the background, but she knew he was there as Ripley, with genuine apology in his voice, gave a gentle and impassioned plea for her to honor him in matrimony. Speechless, Lessy had fled from the sight and had been lying across her bed crying her heart out ever since.

Her mother seemed less concerned than entertained. "Lord-a-mercy, I've never seen that Vassar in such a lather as at the supper table. If looks were bullets, that Ripley boy would have more holes in him than a sieve."

Nora Green, clad in her nightgown, stood before the mirror at the washbowl and combed the tangles out of her long gray hair as she listened to her daughter's pitiful sniveling.

"I can't marry Ripley, Mammy," Lessy declared adamantly. "He's funny and sweet, but I just don't love him."

"Well, of course you don't," her mother agreed easily. "You love Vassar and you have ever since you laid eyes on him."

Her mother's words started Lessy wailing again. "But Vass doesn't want me, not now. Maybe he never has. He never saw the real me, just the perfect angel I pretended to be." The words were a pitiful whine that ended with Lessy face-buried in the quilt. "I tried to tell him in the orchard, to confess at last about how I'd tried to trick him, but he wouldn't listen."

In fury and frustration Lessy pounded the feather tick beneath her. "I can't believe I was so foolish! It was as if I'd taken leave of my senses completely."

Raising her tear-stained face to her mother, she admitted her culpability. "I just wanted to know if

I was pretty enough," she said, shamefaced. "I wanted to know if I could attract a man on my own. If maybe I could have attracted Vass for *me*. Oh, Mammy, I want him to want me for... well, not for my hard work and my high morals, to want me for... oh, for sweet things and sinful things."

Nora Green lay the brush on the chiffonier and moved to the bed, where she knelt and began rubbing her daughter's back in the strong circular motion that had comforted her daughter when she was still a baby.

"Lessy, Lessy," she told her coaxingly. "There is nothing sinful about wanting your man to desire you. And nothing unnatural about wanting a little bit of romance. The man you marry must see more in you than a strong back and a willing hand."

"But that is exactly what he does see. It's all that I've let him see."

Shaking her head, Mammy didn't agree. "If he'd known you for only a few months of this *perfect pretense* you've been putting on, then I'd worry. But no one can keep up a lie for four years! The truth about who you are comes shining through you every day, in the way you move and the songs you sing. Believe me, even if his eyes don't see you as you really are, his heart does."

Lessy looked at her mother, wanting desperately to believe her. "But I've ruined everything,

Mammy," she said. "I've kissed Ripley, and now Vass wants me to marry him."

"Pooh!" Nora waved away the complication. "That load of manure smells to high heaven. Vassar Muldrow wants you for himself. He thinks *you* want that Ripley fellow. And the only way he's going to know any different is if you swallow your pride and tell him yourself."

Lessy's breath caught in a shuddering sigh.

"But the kiss, Mammy?"

"What about the kiss?"

Lessy's cheeks were flushed with shame. "I liked it, Mammy," she said. "I liked it a lot."

Nora rested her chin in her palm thoughtfully. "Did you want it to go on forever?"

"Forever? No."

"Did you feel like you were home at last?"

"Home? We were in the peach orchard."

"Did your heart tell you that you couldn't live without that man?"

Lessy blushed and shook her head. "No, Mammy. My heart kept wishing it was Vassar who kissed like that."

Nora grinned, her expression now completely unconcerned as she shrugged. "That Ripley is the kind of fellow that's been with lots of women, Lessy. A man may learn a few tricks about kissing women that way. Now, maybe your Vass ain't as wise in loving ways. But it ain't an unpleasant study, and I'm thinking you two could learn together."

Lessy swallowed hopefully. "Do you think so, Mammy? Do you think Vass could learn to kiss me like that?"

Her mother chuckled. "I suspect he'd be willing to die trying."

For the first time in hours, Lessy smiled. Maybe things were not as hopeless as they had seemed.

"Of course he'll learn to kiss me like that when we're wed," Lessy assured herself happily. "Why, he's so fine and upstanding, I don't suppose that Vass has ever kissed a woman before in his life."

Out of the comer of her eye Lessy caught a strange expression on her mother's face. "What is it, Mammy?"

Nora began readying herself for bed as if she hadn't heard Lessy's question.

"Mammy?" Lessy's tone was insistent.

Hesitating, as if weighing her words, Nora Green finally shook her head. "I think that he has."

"You think that he's kissed women before?"

"Yes." Her answer was firm and simple, but there was something in her mother's tone of voice that prompted questions in Lessy's mind.

"What is it, Mammy? Is there something you should tell me?"

Sighing heavily before she answered, Lessy's mother seemed clearly unhappy about the revelation she was about to make. "I understand from Jake that the main reason he wanted Vass to come out here and work for us was to separate him from a woman."

Lessy's eyes widened with surprise, and a lump of anxiety settled in the back of her throat. "He was in love with another woman?"

"I don't know if he loved her. He was... ah, seeing her."

Jealousy warred with confusion in Lessy's mind. "Why didn't he marry her? Did Cousin Jake not approve of the match?"

Lessy's mother cleared her throat nervously and looked her daughter straight in the eye. Nora hoped she was ready for the truth. "I don't believe it was possible to approve or disapprove, Lessy. The woman was already married."

Staring at her mother in stunned silence for several seconds, a tiny puff of disbelief emerged from Lessy's mouth before she rolled over on her back to contemplate the ceiling.

"Vassar Muldrow and a married woman." She whispered the words incredulously. Her Vass, the purest of souls, the finest of men, the noblest of the breed, carousing with another man's wife. It was a shock. She didn't know him any better than he knew her.

Her mother blew out the lamp before coming to bed. With a gesture of her hand she urged Lessy to her own side of the bed and crawled in to tuck them both in for the night. "He was young, Lessy, and it was a long time in the past. These things happen sometimes in life," she told her daughter in a sympathetic whisper. "It's best neither to judge nor ruminate. Just put the past behind you and go on. Like that kiss you shared with young Ripley, it was a mistake better outlived and forgotten."

"We don't know each other at all," Lessy whispered, her gaze still focused on the dark ceiling above her.

CHAPTER 7

Vass saw her bringing the water bucket when she was still half a hayfield away. He'd tried to avoid her for the last three days, and he'd managed to do a pretty good job of it. The woman he'd hoped to marry just a week ago had become a polite stranger, and he supposed it was all for the best.

He began moving away from the group. He didn't want to be close when she dipped water for Ripley. He didn't want to see them laughing, their heads together like happy children. He wanted her to be happy. But wanting her to be happy and watching her be that way with another man were not the same thing.

The bright gold of newly cut hay touched the

deep summer blue of the sky behind her. Lessy was like a painted picture on a feed calendar. In his heart she had never looked more beautiful. And she did walk as if she floated off the ground, Vass thought to himself. And then hated that it was Ripley who had pointed it out to him.

He turned away from the sight of her and began hand-raking a long swath of alfalfa. There was a tiredness in his movements. He hadn't slept well for days. He'd always wondered what the early mornings were really like, and now he knew for sure. Frequently he was still awake when they arrived.

The hay was nearly all in the barn. By this time tomorrow the crew would be gone. Would Ripley be staying here with them? Or would he be taking Lessy with him until the season was done? He hoped it was the latter. Within a month he could get things in order and head back to Arkadelphia. He didn't think he could stand to live even a day at this farm with Lessy as a bride to another man.

Strangely his thoughts flew to Mabel Brightmore. Not to sweet memories of illicit indiscretion or wild stories of misspent youth, but to the pain he'd caused her poor old husband. For the first time he thought past his own sin to the pain Brightmore must have felt knowing another man claimed his woman's love. Now he, too, felt that pain.

"I brought you some water."

Vass started at the voice behind him and turned to see Lessy, her hair tucked in a bright blue bonnet smiling up at him in her so-familiar fashion.

He glanced over at the other men.

"Oh, I left them a bucket," Lessy said, guessing his thoughts. "But I brought this jar for you."

"Thank you," Vass said quietly. "But you needn't have gone to the trouble."

"I wouldn't have if I'd thought you'd stay near the men to get a drink, but you've been avoiding me so much, I was afraid you might be fainting in the field from thirst." Her complaint was warm with teasing.

Vass smiled, slightly embarrassed, then took a long drink from the blue quart jar that Lessy handed him.

"It's good," he said, as if the comment were a compliment to her cooking.

With a sigh, Lessy nodded her thanks.

The two looked at each other for long moments, each wishing for something important to say. They had always talked. The farm, the future, the day-to-day workings of life, had come easily to their tongues. But they had never talked about anything important. They had never talked about the feelings they held inside. Now, in his heart, Vass knew that any words were too little and too late. He had never deserved her. He would never be worthy of her, but he did still want her. Vass now wished he'd thrown caution to the wind.

But she'd turned to another man. The fact jolted him back into his sad reality, and he took another swig from the jar just to occupy himself.

"I'm not marrying Ripley," Lessy announced calmly, although her hands were shaking.

Vassar's heart stopped for an instant, and his eyes widened in surprise. Then they narrowed in anger. "Is that no-account trying to worm his way out?"

Lessy sighed and shook her head. "No, he still wants to wed." She laughed lightly. "I don't know what you said to the man, Vass, but you've sure put the fear of God in him. He seems almost desperate to marry me." She took a deep breath before looking him straight in the eyes. "But I'm not having him, not now, not ever."

His expression lightened slightly, but concern was still evident in his features. "I know how you must worry," he said. "But I'm sure that he cares for you. How could he not? And he's not so bad a fellow, and those rounder ways, well, for certain,

Lessy, he's the kind of man to give them up when he's wed."

"I'm not worried about his rounder ways," Lessy said. "I just don't love him."

She was so matter-of-fact that Vass was momentarily taken aback.

"Of course you do," he insisted.

"No, I don't, Vass. I simply don't. Why would you think so?"

"I saw you in the peach orchard, Lessy," he said quietly. "I know you. And you're not the kind of woman to ... well."

Lessy's cheeks were bright red with embarrassment, but she bravely bit her lip before she spoke. "That's what you don't understand about me, Vass. I am exactly that kind of woman. I am exactly the kind of woman to do all kinds of silly foolishness. I'm just a regular, ordinary woman with as many faults as any of my gender."

"What do you mean?"

"I tried to tell you that day, Vass. I am not the sweet, hardworking young farm woman who thinks everything you think and wants everything that you want. That's just what I've pretended to be."

"You are perfect," Vass told her.

"No, Vass. Truth is, I'm far from perfect. Before you came I was as averse to chores as any other farm girl. I could hardly wait for Sundays to see my friends, and I spent my free time with them laughing and gossiping and getting into foolishness. I don't want to spend my peach money on waterfowl for the pond. I want the fanciest silk wedding dress this county has ever seen. And I want to be kissed and sparked and spooned along the edges before I'm safely wed. And if the man I love isn't willing, I am certainly weak enough that another man will do."

Vass saw the tears that had formed in her eyes, and he knew he should reach to comfort her, but he was frozen in place.

"I love you and I have since the first day you drove up in the yard. And I tried to be perfect for you, Vassar, because I believed that you were perfect. I assured myself that you could never want me as myself, so I made myself become someone else. Someone as perfect as I believed that you were. Daddy used to tell me that my life was like bread dough. I could shape it and form it into anything I ever wanted. And he was right about that, Vass. I just didn't understand that I would still be bread even if I fashioned myself as a heart of gold. I can't be perfect for you, Vassar."

He lifted his hands, denying her words. "Lessy, I'm not perfect myself."

"I know that, Vass," she said. "You like to sleep late, and you're a little single-minded at times, and you work too hard. I was so busy loving you that I blinded myself to your faults and your weaknesses as I wanted to blind you to my own. But I cannot blind myself to the fact that you don't seem to want me, Vass. You don't want me as a man wants a woman."

He swallowed hard. Her confession was frightening in its erroneousness, its honesty, and its potential. Maybe it was not over. Could there still be a chance for him to have the woman that he loved?

"I have more faults, Lessy, than those you've mentioned," he said evenly. "I have a . .. well... a weakness for women that I've tried not to show you."

Lessy looked up into his eyes, still trusting. "Mammy told me about your 'woman trouble' in Arkadelphia," she said. "It's truly none of my business, but I wished that I'd known it sooner. Then maybe I would have realized that it wasn't my own, very human nature that kept you at a distance, but your own lack of desire for me."

Vassar's face was rigid.

"You wanted a good little farm wife that would do everything right but wouldn't press on your heart, wouldn't demand your love in return. Do you still carry a torch for that married woman in your past?"

He shook his head. “No! Lessy, of course I don’t.”

Lessy nodded only slightly. “Well, I am glad about that, I suppose.” She swallowed bravely. “I’ve already said that I love you, and I can tell you now that I always will. I just wish that you had a weakness for me the way you had a weakness for her. That’s what I came out here to tell you after all.” Her chin was raised with challenge, and her stance was willful with her arms folded stubbornly across her chest.

“I may never wed. I may live my whole life as an unloved, dried-up old maid. But I’d rather do that than have a man that I’d have to pretend with. Or a man that would have to pretend to wanting me.”

Eyes narrowing in anger, Lessy jerked the mason jar out of his hand. Fury stiffened her spine as she turned to go. Vass stared after her with stunned disbelief. Who was this wild fiery woman who was living in sweet little Lessy’s body? Who was spitting fire at him from soft-spoken little Lessy’s mouth? Who was stomping angrily away across the hayfield, the soft floating walk of Lessy now an alluring sultry sway of hips that enticed him with every step?

“Lessy!”

His call stopped her dead still, but she didn’t

turn around. Vassar began to run. Standing stiffly in the field, she didn't once look back as he called her name over and over as he raced toward her. Reaching her side, he grabbed her arm and pulled her toward him. His heart pounded in his chest as he drew her to face him.

"Lessy." He spoke only a little above a whisper.

"Vassar," she answered, her voice as quiet as his own.

A thousand thoughts jumbled in his mind. A thousand excuses and a thousand explanations jockeyed for first confession from his tongue. But the words that came out were from the heart, not the head.

"I love you, Lessy. I love you. I haven't given more than a thought to Mabel Brightmore since the day I came to this farm. I want you, Lessy. How can you ever doubt it? I can't get up in the morning because I spend all night long dreaming that I hold you in my arms." His eyes burned with a feverish glow. "Make that dream come true for me, Lessy," he whispered. "Take me, boring, slugabed, and all, and I will spend the rest of my life learning to love you for who you really are."

He leaned forward and wrapped his arms about her waist. "I love you, Lessy," he said. "I love you whoever you are."

Pulling her close, Vass lowered his mouth to

hers. It was a kiss of fire, a kiss of desperation, a kiss of passion. Lessy's own arms circled his neck and pulled him even closer as she answered the question in his touch. His lips were greedy, eager, starving at her mouth, and he could not pull her near enough to ease the ache that gnawed at him.

Lessy, too, felt her flesh jittering like lightning in the clouds of a summer storm. She couldn't keep her hands still as they wandered the wide breadth of his shoulders and caressed the soft blond hair at the nape of his neck.

One of Vassar's big sun-browned hands slipped low on her back and pressed her more tightly against him. He rubbed himself against her in a rough and lusty manner, and her own eager response and moan of shocked delight urged him on.

Vass broke the kiss from her mouth to trail his lips along her throat. Greedily his tongue flickered against the tiny marks on the underside of her jaw that had long lured him. He pressed her bosom tightly to his chest, feeling her soft tempting roundness and the hard, eager nipples. Struggling valiantly he managed to get exploring fingers between his heated flesh and her own.

Lessy threw her head back in delight and bit down painfully on her lip, trying to control the waves of pleasure that were coursing through her.

Vassar's other hand slid down her backside,

clutching her bottom and squeezing her gently before venturing down the back of her thigh.

Pressing his face against her bosom, he heard and felt the rapid pounding of her heart. She wanted him as he wanted her. And he was loath to wait another minute.

He dropped to his knees in front of her and lay his cheek gently against the soft curve of her belly. Here she would receive his love, and here she would carry his children. He pressed his lips to the warm soft cotton of her skirt for one long struggling moment of thrilling enticement before he raised his eyes to hers.

He fought for breath and the right words to say as he took her hands in his own. Bringing her knuckles to his lips, he kissed them ardently, submissively, like a slave to a queen.

"Do you believe now that I want you, Lessy? Can you doubt it?"

He ran his hands eagerly along her thighs, and her eyes widened in shock and wicked delight.

"Marry me, Lessy," he pleaded. "Marry me and allow me to learn everything there is to know about the woman that I love. Marry me and find out the truth about the man who has dreamed of being your husband since the day that we met."

Lessy dropped to her knees beside him in the grass and whispered yes as again they embraced.

Unashamedly they kissed and caressed each other in the blind passion of new love. Lessy trembled at his touch, and Vass struggled with control as the flame of their love set the kindling of desire to blaze.

Vass would have laid with her, there in the fresh-mown hay of the summer afternoon, and she would have let him. There was no shame or sin in what they felt. Vows unspoken had already been said with the heart.

But the hoots and hollers of a rowdy haying crew penetrated their blissful heaven, causing them to jerk away from each other in disbelief and embarrassment.

"The men!" Lessy squealed shamefaced as she hastily pulled together her bodice that inexplicably had come undone.

Vass hurriedly moved in front of her to shield her from the eyes of the yammering yahoos waving and shouting from near the hay wagon.

"I forgot that they were there," Lessy admitted and then foolishly began to giggle.

Vass caught her mood and chuckled, also, before shaking his head with self-derision. "I swear, Lessy. I forgot that there was anyone else in the whole world."

EPILOGUE

The train shuddered to a stop at the new clapboard station. The porter put down a block of steps, and two young children scampered down from the train followed by Lessy and Vassar Muldrow.

"Lena June!" Lessy called out to the little girl. "Mind your brother while your daddy and I get the bags."

The porter handed down two well-worn grip sacks and received both a tip and a thank you from Vass.

Lessy looked around the clean, modem new station in a town that hadn't even existed when the two had taken their first trip, their honeymoon trip, nearly eight years ago.

Theirs had been the fanciest wedding that the county had ever seen. Vassar had worn a brand-new suit that was swell enough to get buried in. His dad and brothers had made the trip from Arkadelphia to stand up with him. And both his mother and Mammy Green had worn new store-bought dresses from Kansas City.

Lessy's fine white gown had been silk and lace, which she had fancifully embroidered with tiny ducks and geese around the bodice and hem.

They had delayed the wedding several weeks to come up with all the finery, including satin ribbons on the church pews and dripless candles of pure white from the Montgomery Ward catalog.

"We are only going to marry once," Vass had said. "We want the public symbol of it to be as special as our private happiness."

Poor Reverend Watson had become a little anxious for the day to arrive. The young couple had become so calf-eyed and openly affectionate, they had become a near scandal and a clear embarrassment to the community. Lessy giggled even now at the memory of the hang-dog expression that had been on Vass's face those last few nights when they'd had to part at bedtime.

Finally, when they'd stepped out of the church, laughing and delighted to be Mr. and Mrs. Vassar Muldrow, he'd lifted Lessy clear off the ground and twirled her around like a whirligig until they were both laughing and dizzy and the congregation thought them half crazy. With almost discourteous haste, they'd made their getaway in the brightly festooned buggy as if they could hardly wait for the privacy of their honeymoon Pullman car to Kansas City.

"What are you thinking about, Lessy?" Vassar asked as he managed to grasp both bags in one hand and chivalrously took her arm. "You've got a faraway look on that face I know so well."

She grinned suggestively. "It's so nice to be able to ride the train all the way home," she said. "My least favorite part of our yearly vacations was always that long buggy ride home from DeQueen."

"That buggy ride was downright romantic until we had two wild Indians that we have to practically tie to the buggy."

Lessy smiled wryly and nodded agreement.

'Tommy, Lena June, don't go running off," he called sternly after the children, who seemed much in danger of doing exactly that.

As the couple made their way off the platform, to the newly bricked street that was the pride of the brand-new town, the children followed in their fashion. With a blast of whistle and a smoky puff of steam, the train headed on down the track to Texarkana.

"Look, Daddy!" the little boy squealed, pointing a chubby finger at a new, brightly colored billboard next to the station.

The two adults surveyed the signboard as Lessy read it aloud. " 'Welcome to Peach Grove, Arkansas. Population 1,895. Home of Ripley-Muldrow Agricultural Works. Arkansas Machines for American Farmers.' "

"That's our name!" young Tom exclaimed with a delighted giggle.

Vass gave a wry grin and a long-suffering sigh. 'That Rip can never seem to remember the 'silent' in 'silent partner.' "

Lessy waved away his objection. "It's a good name. You *are* the one who helped him get started."

Vass shook his head. "We've received plenty of compensation for that over the years. It was only a little investment that paid off. It was Rip's business, his designs, and his hard work that made the company and gave this little community a bit of commerce and enterprise aside from farming."

Lessy couldn't argue that.

"He should have called it Ripley and Sons," Vass said firmly.

Lessy giggled at his affronted puffiness. "That would have been a good name for it, considering all the sons that he has. It seems like poor Sugie Jo is in the family way nearly all the time."

Vass grinned. "And such big boys they are, too." His eyes were wide with feigned innocence. "Why, that oldest of theirs, nearly nine and a half pounds the day he was born! And a full three months early at that."

"Vassar!" Lessy hissed through her teeth. "The children."

Her discomfiture only brought a deep chuckle and a broader smile to his face. "Now, Lessy honey, don't be acting all proper and saintly on me now. If there is one thing I've learned about the woman that I've married, it's that she is plainly just as fraught with human frailties as I am."

As the children moved on up ahead of them, Vassar began to hum a familiar tune, and taking up the challenge, Lessy joined in, quietly singing the bawdy words that her husband had taught her and that she now knew by heart.

"She was curved and plump
And broad of rump
And her drawers were pink and frilly.
As years may pass, I'll oft recall
That day spent plowing Millie."

ALSO BY PAMELA MORSI

Territory Trysts

Wild Oats

Runabout

Tales from Marrying Stone

Marrying Stone

Simple Jess

The Lovesick Cure

A Marrying Stone Christmas (coming soon)

Small-Town Swains

Heaven Sent

Something Shady

No Ordinary Princess

Sealed With a Kiss

Garters

The Love Charm

Women's Fiction

Doing Good/Social Climber of Davenport Heights

Letting Go

Suburban Renewal

By Summer's End

The Cotton Queen

Bitsy's Bait & BBQ

Last Dance at Jitterbug Lounge

Red's Hot Honky-Tonk Bar

Contemporary Romance

The Bikini Car Wash

The Bentley's Buy at Buick

Love Overdue

Mr. Right Goes Wrong

Single Title Historicals

Courting Miss Hattie

Sweetwood Bride

Here Comes the Bride

Novellas

With Marriage In Mind in the collection *Matters of the Heart*

The Pantry Raid in the collection *The Night We Met*

Daffodils In Spring in the collection *More Than Words: Where Dreams Begin*

Making Hay

ABOUT THE AUTHOR

National bestseller and two-time RITA Award winner, Pamela Morsi was duly warned. "Lots of people mistakenly think they are writers," her mother told her. She'd be smart to give it up before she embarrassed herself. Fortunately, she rarely took her mother's advice. With 30 published titles and millions of copies in print, she loves to hear from readers at her website @ pamelamorsi.com

More places to connect with Pam:

Made in the USA
Coppell, TX
02 November 2020

40647699R00080